W9-AVR-397

SHOPPING FOR A BILLIONAIRE'S FIANCÉE

(DECLAN'S PROPOSAL)

BY JULIA KENT

Copyright © 2015 by Julia Kent

ALL RIGHTS RESERVED. This book contains material protected under International and Federal Copyright Laws and Treaties. Any unauthorized reprint or use of this material is prohibited. No part of this book may be reproduced or transmitted in any form or by any means, electronic or mechanical, including photocopying, recording, or by any information storage and retrieval system without express written permission from the author / publisher.

* * *

Sign up for my New Releases and Sales newsletter at http://www.jkentauthor.com

TABLE OF CONTENTS

Praise for Julia Kent

From Authors

"This one has it all: hilarious laughs, a sexy (almost) billionaire and a hint of tears. The best of the series!"
—Celia Kyle, *New York Times* bestselling romantic comedy author

"Her stories are sensual, incredible, and outright hilarious—the PERFECT combination."
—Sara Fawkes, *New York Times* bestselling author of the *Anything He Wants* series

"If you like ... romances ... with lots of humor, this is the series for you!"
—Mimi Strong, *New York Times* bestselling romantic comedy author

"Julia Kent's romantic comedies are so funny you'll snort soda out your nose, so emotionally honest you'll get misty eyed, and so charming you'll be back for more. Loved the whole series!"
—Cheri Allan, author of the *Betting on Romance* series

Reader Reviews

"This book is not to be missed!!!"

"Wow Julia has done it again!! This book had me on edge with the suspense and overwhelmed with laughter at times! I even cried a little. I absolutely love this series!!! I can't wait to see what's to come next!!! This is a must read!"

"Every chapter made my heart beat faster in anticipation. Julia Kent once again pulls at our emotions and allows us to fall in love with the characters all over again.... Very well worth my heart palpitations."

Reader Emails

"I just can't imagine how you come up with this stuff, but am so glad you do!"

"I finally had to write to you and tell you that you are simply one of the most amazing authors. Your humor is perfect. I really do bust out laughing out loud. My family thinks that I am crazy when I do it but I can count on a good read from you especially when it has been a rough day. There hasn't been a single thing that you have written that I haven't fallen in love with the characters. They become real and some of your lines have become a part of our family language. Thank you for sharing your amazing gift."

"Having another fantastic evening as I just finished your latest book and now the fam can go to sleep since the laughing/screaming out loud has stopped... Stomach muscles are sore. Better than sit-ups! :-)"

All of our best dates end up in the emergency room....

I planned the perfect proposal. Plenty of lobster, caviar, champagne and—her favorite—tiramisu. The perfect setting. The perfect woman.

The perfect *everything*.

Dad gave me my late mother's engagement ring, platinum and diamonds galore. Shannon wouldn't care if I slid a giant hard-candy ring on her finger instead of a three-carat diamond designed to impress.

But my future mother-in-law, Marie, will pass out when she sets eyes on that rock, and that will give us two minutes of blessed silence. That woman talks more than Kim Kardashian flashes her naked backside on the internet.

I was going to make it perfect, from the color of the tablecloth to the freshness of the roses.

And it *was* perfect.

Until Shannon swallowed the ring.

* * *

Shopping for a Billionaire's Fiancée gives near-billionaire Declan McCormick the chance to tell his story in this continuation of the New York Times and USA Today bestselling *Shopping for a Billionaire* series.

CHAPTER ONE

Shannon has no idea how many layers of beauty she has. And that's exactly why she's so exquisite.

When I was sixteen, the year before my mother died, Mom took me and my little brother, Andrew, to New York City for a long weekend. Pulled us out of school over the objections of the headmaster at our academy. Mom didn't care. We spent three nights at the Waldorf Astoria, skated at Rockefeller Center, had the best seats at the top Broadway musicals, and dined on the finest footlongs you could get for $3. Loaded with mustard and sauerkraut, plus a cream soda or two.

(Do you have something against footlongs? Too bad. Two teenagers can only handle so much caviar and lobster.)

What I remember most about that trip, and what Shannon reminds me of every moment I look at her, was our trip to the Museum of Modern Art. Mom insisted we go, and Andrew and I rolled our eyes like sets of dice at a craps table.

And then.

And then I *got* it, right there in front of a Vincent van Gogh masterpiece. In art history class we'd covered this painting in detail. We were taught the biography of Van Gogh, how he came to create the series of paintings, his motivation, and his flaws.

We'd dissected the meaning so thoroughly that I felt like I could recreate the art by automation, our elite prep-school instruction clinical and impeccable.

Standing in front of the painting, a few feet away, with my eyes trailing the curve of brush strokes, my mind taking in the nuance of color, my senses dazzled by the sheer essence of the whole, I halted. Froze. Was completely in the painting's spell.

You can study something in the abstract. Know it's real somewhere out there in the world, and understand intellectually that what you read in a book or what you're told by someone else is true.

You have to stand in front of it and have it stare back at you, though, to really *know* it.

That's how I feel when I look at Shannon. Every single time my eyes find her. Shannon's smile is warm and sweet, yet better every time she flashes it at me. Her honey-colored hair shines in the sunlight but looks richer when it's tangled, in bed, highlighted by the moon and messed by *me*. Those warm eyes see only me when we're together. That luscious body craves my touch. My hands. My...all of it.

When I'm with her, the world is more nuanced. Deeper. Authentic. Real.

She's a work of art, one of a kind. And one I get to hold next to my body, tuck away in my heart, and...grow old with.

I have planned the perfect proposal. No footlongs and sauerkraut, unfortunately, but plenty of lobster, caviar, champagne and—her favorite— tiramisu. (What is it with women and tiramisu? It's cream, cheese, sugar, cake and rum, not some magic potion that generates mouth orgasms. My Y chromosome scratches its head in confusion, but hey, if it's her favorite...I give my woman what she wants.)

Dad gave me Mom's engagement ring, platinum and diamonds galore, a monstrosity he'd bought for her nearly four decades ago as his business took off. The ring is designed to impress. I doubt Shannon would care if I slid a giant hard-candy ring on her finger instead of a three-carat diamond.

And, frankly, *I* don't care, either. But the thought of my Shannon sharing such an important part of my mother's life makes my chest swell. Only Shannon—and my mom—can do that. Only love can do that.

Plus, Marie will pass out when she sets eyes on that rock, and that will give us two minutes of blessed silence. That woman talks more than Kim Kardashian flashes her naked ass on the internet.

"It's not as if your brothers are planning to tie themselves down to one woman any time soon, if ever," Dad had said when he gave it to me. He's about as sentimental as a pet rock. After having it resized to fit my future fiancée, it was ready to rest on yet another McCormick woman's finger.

It was going to be calculatedly perfect, down to the color of the tablecloth and the freshness of the roses.

And it *was* perfect.

Until Shannon swallowed the ring.

Why do all our best dates end up at the ER?

And who the hell called her mother?

CHAPTER TWO

One week before the proposal...

Grace taps her knuckles on my doorway. For some reason, the door is ajar, the muffled sounds of copiers buzzing and people talking to each other a dull roar in the distance. They all annoy me.

"Declan? The jeweler called. The ring is ready."

My blank stare is all I can muster.

She smiles. "Are *you?*"

"Am I what?"

"Ready." Grace looks like she could get into a catfight with Honey Boo Boo's mom and come out the winner. When she frowns, something deep and primal in me clenches.

That's why she's the best damned admin a guy could have. No worries about office sex (Grace is a lesbian married to a rugby player) and in a pinch, she can act as a bodyguard.

"Ready for a meeting?" Based on the look she gives me, I am not with the program this morning. Frankly, I am not on the planet this morning. Between a helicopter ride from New York that was so choppy I might as well have been riding a bucking bronco, and no sex at all from Shannon for three entire days (due to business meetings in NYC), I am lucky I can read a basic stock report and tie my shoes.

"Ready to get married."

Oh. Yeah. And then there's *that*.

Did I mention the no sex part? Because that's really occupying my addled brain more than the whole pick-one-woman-for-the-rest-of-your-life thing.

And only one woman.

One.

It's not so hard to pick one woman to be with for all eternity, right? Grace did it, so I can, too. "Yeah. I'm ready."

"You look sick. Not 'ready'." Grace steps in my office all the way and gently closes the door, holding the doorknob like it's a ticking time bomb, waiting for the gentle click before turning to me with that look.

You know that look. The look older women give you, their eyes going soft and concerned, like you deserve to be the object of pity, the recipient of chicken soup and completely unusable advice.

Three thin, gold bracelets jangle against her freckled, wrinkled skin. She's nothing like my future mother-in-law, and—

My entire body tenses for no apparent reason whatsoever. It's as if the Ghost of Testosterone Past has slipped into my office unannounced.

Future mother-in-law.

Marie.

"I'm fine," I insist. This is getting old. I have three video conferences with accounts, a business lunch with a client who thinks tequila shots confer the same health benefits as a field green salad (and by the fourth shot, I always agree with him), and a woman right here in this building who I need to locate, pull into a supply closet and bang senseless.

(That would be *Shannon*, for the record.)

"Declan, I've known you since you were in high school, and I'm going to take off my admin hat for a moment and put on my not-quite-mother hat," Grace says, complete with hand gestures, as if she's pretending to wear a hat.

Grace was a pre-school teacher in her first career. It shows.

"I have enough not-quite-mothers in my life," I say in the most *I am annoyed* voice I can manage, which is a pretty damn strong one. Shannon tells me I have Resting Asshole Face. It's like Resting Bitchface but for men.

I try it out on Grace right now.

She waves me off. "Oh, stop it. Listen to me. You're about to propose to the woman you love. Any man in your shoes would be nervous."

"Nervous," I scoff, standing up and buttoning my suit jacket, unbuttoning it, buttoning it. The buttons are a bit tight and it just came back from the tailor for readjustment. I am not nervous.

"You're human, Declan."

"I'm a McCormick. We're not allowed to be human."

"No matter how often your father says that, you know it's not true," Grace says with a smile, clasping her hands in front of her, making the gold at her wrists jingle again.

Someone knocks on the door. We both turn and look.

"Come in," I call out. To Grace, I mutter, "Maybe we're secret immortal werewolves and we've fooled you."

"You're too vain about your suits to let them get torn when you shift," says Shannon, entering the room with a smile.

One part of my clothing threatens to split quite suddenly.

Grace gives me a look that says *We're not done here*. Oh, yes, we are. We're done talking about whether I'm ready for marriage and, instead, we're going to talk about how ready I am for sex.

If we're measuring that readiness, it's a good nine inches long.

(You expect me to be modest? Good luck with that. Facts are facts.)

Shannon works three floors below me. I like knowing she's under me all the time. Right now, I want her on top of me, beneath me, spooned in front of me, on her knees at my feet...hell, I'll take anything. I can hear my heart beat in the quiet between us, except the blood isn't pounding through my chest right now.

Grace departs, and I take in the vision of my future bride. *Bride*. I like that word. Could get used to saying it, especially since it has the word "ride" tucked right in there.

Shannon. My *ride*.

She's wearing a dark grey suit with a double-breasted jacket and a light colored shirt under it. Nylons and high heels a little taller than the ones she normally wears. Her brown hair is pulled back in a braid, her lips freshly painted with bright red lipstick. Long lashes frame those perfect eyes. Shannon is working the hell out of the naughty librarian look.

She moves toward my desk, not touching me, walking past to tease. She knows damn well how hard I want her, er...how *much* I want her, and she's prolonging the moment, stretching it out in an endless series of sultry moves designed to make me fling every paper off my desk and take her in front of the giant glass windows here on the twenty-second floor, with a view of the Back Bay our orgasmic scenery.

The seam of my zipper begins to split as she pulls herself up to sit on the edge of my desk, slipping her heels off with stocking feet, and she widens her legs.

Garters. *Red* garters. And—

My inner werewolf is trying to climb out of my body through my pants fly.

She's wearing no panties. At all. Shannon doesn't *do* this.

Oh, thank God she's doing this.

"See something you like, Mr. McCormick? I'm here to pitch a new product for you to consider for Anterdec Holdings." Widening her legs even more, she licks those red lips. The lipstick matches the color of the garters.

"A new product?" I say through a mouth full of marbles and dead brain cells, hands burning to touch her. I take a step forward and pause, letting desire wash over me. Better enjoy it for a second or two, because in three seconds I'll be inside her.

"Yes," she says, unbuttoning her suit jacket, leaning back on the desk with her arms. She's wearing a red corset.

Corset. A corset makes gravity its bitch. The engineering behind this simple piece of clothing deserves the Nobel Peace Prize, because there is nothing in the world—nothing—that will get a group of straight men to share the same opinion than the sight of a woman in a red corset.

"Nice," I groan. Her breasts are pushed up, abundant and in need of release. The last time I saw her looking so wicked was at Christmas, eight months ago, when she wore an elf costume that made me deliver Shannon a sack full of goodies.

And by "sack," I mean—

Bzzzz.

You've got to be kidding me.

Shannon sits up and—no! Don't cross your arms like that and put the Himalayas away!

"Declan?" It's Grace, over my phone's intercom. Dad insists on keeping this charming 1970s ritual. Says it makes him feel like some guy from an old television show about three gorgeous female private investigators. Right now, I'm about to grab the phone and throw it out the window.

"Yes? It better be important," I say as I march toward Shannon, nudging her knees back to their proper, wide position, my hands hot on her waist. She looks uncertain, and I need to kiss that out of her.

"Shh!" Shannon whispers in my ear. "I don't want her to think that we...that you and I are...you know."

"We're *not*," I groan. "That's the problem."

"Declan, there's a call for you. From New Zealand. Says it's important. Something to do with a marketing campaign that's glitching because of faulty web software." Grace's voice crackles like we're on a police radio.

I look at the clock. "It's the middle of the night there! Who cares if people can't get their custom-blend cosmetics for the new spa line?" Anterdec handles a chain of twenty-three luxury hotels and spas in New Zealand. We're rolling out a new product line. In exchange for giving me Mom's engagement ring, Dad got a concession out of me: fix the nightmare project in New Zealand. What had started out as a nice, cushy contract had turned into an international disaster. I'd left the project a year ago in fabulous shape and it had disintegrated. The developers assured me that going "live" would be glitchless.

They lied. Developers lie. You know those Dilbert cartoons where the marketing people are portrayed as dunderheads who have no link to logic or reality? Who do you think writes that comic strip?

A developer.

"And you're interrupting me because..."

"Because the system's crashing and customer service is lighting up in Indonesia and—you need to take this call. It's the CEO."

"Fine," I snap. Grace disappears. So does Shannon, wiggling out of my arms and re-buttoning her coat. A whiff of her perfume, light and feminine, tickles my nose. So does her natural scent, those legs open and waiting for me seconds ago, her body primed for me.

All traces of red, except for her lips, vanish as she folds herself back from the unfolding, making her outer package professional again.

One important, throbbing thing of mine doesn't vanish, though. I grab her and pull her to me, the kiss hot and sweet. She tastes like coffee and vanilla, like beeswax and sunshine, the smear of her lipstick making our kiss more urgent. I'm groaning again and I need her.

I can't wait to put that ring on her finger.

I can't wait to see her wearing nothing *but* that ring.

"A quickie?" she whispers, fingers already on my belt buckle, hand feeling exactly how much I've missed her. I know damn well I've picked the perfect woman to marry, because who else offers you sweet relief in the middle of an international software failure? A woman who gets *that* is the woman you want bearing your children.

The intercom coughs. Grace's voice pours out. "Dec? Three calls now from New Zealand, and one from Indonesia. What do I tell them? I'm getting screamed at in two different languages and across three time zones here."

Shannon's hands freeze.

This is brutally unfair.

When I was six, and Terry got to go on a school trip to Disneyworld. It wasn't fair. I cried for three days and begged to be allowed to go, but Dad was too busy with business travel and mergers, while Mom explained ad nauseam that Terry was in the

12

band and was marching in a parade. If that was supposed to make me feel better, it backfired.

I learned that the world just isn't fair.

Shannon's unmoving hands on my belt buckle is a nasty reminder of that lesson.

"Damn," I hiss as she "helps" by re-buckling my belt, tucking my shirt in. Not that there's much room for it. I have the equivalent of a baseball bat in my pants.

She pats the front of my pants in place and smooths it, which is like pouring salt on a shark bite.

"You need to go fix this," she says, reaching up to brush my hair out of my eyes. I keep forgetting to get it cut, and she's asked me to grow it out. Likes the look, she says.

"I need to have you pinned beneath me with those garters giving my kidneys a massage," I growl.

"Later. My place?" She hasn't moved in with me. Yet. Says she wants to wait until we're engaged. Meanwhile, she still shares that tiny little one-bedroom apartment with her sister. Her best friend, Amanda, is like a third roommate, and then there's the Ghost of Crazyass Mothers-in-Law who haunts the place, barging in at will.

I love Marie. I do. I just love her in the abstract.

"*My* place," I grunt. "Not yours. There's no way we're going to try to have sex at your place again. Ever." I frown, and she knows exactly what I mean.

The Incident.

"It won't happen again, you know," she says with a pleading look in her eyes.

"Right. Because I am never having sex with you in your apartment. Ever. Therefore, it will never happen again." The burn of The Incident haunts me. It happened last week.

Just after I decided to propose.

Shannon stops trying to argue. She reaches for a hug and my hand slides up that nice, hot thigh and sinks into—

Oh, sweet Jesus.

"Declan!" she hisses, pulling back, her cheeks as pink as the place I just touched.

"I can't help it." Seriously. I can't. C'mon. I'm a guy. A guy who hasn't had sex in three days. Would you begrudge a three-days-dehydrated man a sip of a water bottle waved like a semaphore flag in front of him?

"Yes, you can." She gives me a quick kiss on the cheek and scampers out, leaving me with people on the phone from the other side of the world ready to scream at me, a hand that touched the gates to Heaven, and a raging hard on.

This is all *someone's* fault.

But none of that matters, because life is unfair, and the only way to deal with it is to keep on living.

And scream back.

CHAPTER THREE

Andrew won't let me get out of this one. "Hold on. Back up. This 'incident' at Shannon's apartment. Say that again? Her mom walked in on you two having sex and *recorded* it? Was it under-the-covers sex or let-your-freak-flag-fly sex?"

"What the hell does it matter? My future mother-in-law saw me naked. You don't recover from that. Ever," I shoot back. And for the record, it's always let-your-freak-flag-fly sex. *Always*.

We're weightlifting. There are two ways to deal with an unwelcome hard on. Masturbate, or go to the gym. Because I have a strict rule about sex at work—it must involve another human being—I'm left with one option.

The gym.

At Anterdec, that means going into Andrew's office and entering a swipe card along a reader installed in the wall. You'd never know the hidden gym is in there. While he's a fitness freak with a spin cycle in his main office, he's also a free-weights nut with a deep fear of being outside because of his deadly wasp allergy.

All I know is I get to work out and pump as much blood as possible out of my pelvis and into my legs and arms. It's the blood immigration program, complete with free relocation and a puppy if you move. After two hours of being yelled at by people with accents that make them sound like they really need to put another shrimp on the barbie and poke a skewer through their eye, I need this. Gym time. Pump out the rage.

Blow out my muscles.

The words *pump* and *blow* are killing me, though. Shannon got called across town for a client meeting and swears she'll meet me at eight o'clock tonight in my apartment. If she's not there at exactly eight, I'm sending out a search party led by a one-eyed trouser snake.

I'm sure Jessica Coffin will have a field day tweeting that.

Andrew's trying very hard not to snicker. "Marie just barged in to Shannon's bedroom?"

"Yes." I'm lifting forties, working my triceps, on my back on a yoga ball. Andrew grabs them out of my hands and gives me fifty-fives. It takes effort, but I can still press them. I imagine the blood fleeing into my arms.

Too bad the desire can't be relocated.

"With a camera crew?" Andrew's standing over me, looking down, eyes filled with the kind of laughter no older brother ever wants to see in his little bro.

"Yep."

"And the camera crew was because..."

"She showed up with the grandsons of one of her yoga clients. That old lady named Agnes."

Andrew touches his ass tenderly. "The pincher?" Marie had convinced him to attend one of her yoga classes a few months ago, by promising a direct path to the studio in the winter, insect-free.

"Yep." I drop the fifty-fives and motion for the sixties. Andrew hands them off and chugs from his water bottle. "Marie said they were doing a documentary on her."

"*Marie?* Why? Is she some kind of celebrity?"

"The local cable access channel was doing some show on her life as a 'reinvented woman' who found a new career in her fifties, and she wanted them to shadow her as she visited her kids."

We'd been so deeply, intensely involved in being naked and sticky and perfect that we hadn't heard the front door open. Then *bam!* A doorway full of Marie and chattering and screams and shoving, and all I really remember from the whole thing was Chuckles, rubbing his front paws together and doing a Dr. Evil imitation. And shouting, from me. Lots of shouting. Then Shannon, sobbing, and...

Andrew winces. "They caught you doing the two-backed nasty on camera?"

"Hey! Don't talk about red garters—er, Shannon like that. That's my future wife you're talking about."

Andrew's jaw goes slack. "Red garters?" See that thin line of drool running down his mouth, the vacant look in his eyes? Told you. It's Man Soma. Mention garters and we check out, controlled by hormones. Pavlov's bell in lingerie form.

"And a corset."

He groans, a sexual sound that borders on lewd. Then again, among the testicled, this is the expected response, but still.

17

I frown. "Quit thinking about Shannon like that."

"I'm not thinking about *Shannon*."

I sit up. This is new. Andrew doesn't date. Not the way normal people date, at least. Andrew's admin picks socially acceptable women and sets them up for business meetings that start with a handshake and end with a Walk of Shame.

"Who are you thinking about?"

"I'm—Amand—no, no one."

"A *man*?" Oh, boy. This conversation just veered into new territory.

"Not a man! I don't date men."

"It's cool. Not judging if you do. Look at Tim Cook. The CEO of Apple can be out and proud—"

"But I am not gay! I didn't say 'a man'!"

"Yes, you did."

He's flustered. This is fun. Andrew takes a deep breath and runs his hand through increasingly-wet hair. Funny. He hasn't lifted enough to be *that* sweat-soaked. "I said 'aman', not 'a man.'"

"And the difference is..."

"One is a woman and one isn't."

"That makes no sense. What's 'Aman', then?" While I'm waiting for an answer, it hits me. Aman. Amanda. Andrew's got a thing for Shannon's best friend.

"It's Amanda, isn't it?" Most people would keep their mouth shut but he's my little brother. It's in my DNA to torture him. Plus, he's on the fast track to become CEO and Dad picked him. Not me. I have resentment and have to take it out on Andrew somewhere.

"It's no one. Shut up. Spot me while I lift." Andrew is the worst liar. Always has been. He's fine with a poker face when it comes to business, but on a personal level, he's the last person you want to tell a secret.

"Amanda Red Corset Chest," I taunt. Andrew's face tightens. Zing! Hit the target.

He snorts, trying to play this off like it's nothing. "I wouldn't know Amanda if I walked past her on the street. Haven't seen her in what...fourteen months?"

Right. He wouldn't know her if he passed her on the street. But who's counting?

Oh. *He* is. How many months it's been since he saw her. I know *I*, personally, keep track of how many months it's been since I last saw someone I don't give two shits about.

Not.

"Let's talk about your future mother-in-law getting a full-on view of your ass and...hey. Wait a minute." He folds his legs and sits on the ground next to me. I'm still on the plastic yoga ball, now stretching out my hips.

"Did you say the words 'future wife'?" he asks. Sweat is pouring off him and he wipes it off his neck with a small hand towel.

"Yes."

"You're *proposing*? To Shannon?"

"No, to Marie. Thought I'd kidnap her and run off into the sunset."

"You have a thing for fifty-something buxom blondes with sex fetishes?"

"Can we stop talking about 'sex' and 'Marie' in the same sentence?" I snap. At least this conversation has taken care of my hard on. It's long gone, like Mitt Romney's chances of becoming president.

"Marriage, huh? You feel ready for that? One woman for the rest of your life?"

"Why does everyone keep bringing up the *one woman* thing?"

"Because your reputation precedes you."

"What reputation?" I know what he means and brace myself.

"Remember what Jessica said once? How you managed through sheer force of will to make 'Declan' rhyme with 'man whore'?" He frowns and stands up, reaching for a hand towel. As he wipes his neck he asks, "Does Shannon know?"

"You mean, have we shared our numbers?"

"Yes."

I nod.

"And did you have to bring out the quantum computer to calculate yours, while she used one hand for hers?"

"She uses one hand very well."

Andrew leers and I regret the comment instantly.

"If we're going to talk about sex and numbers, how was your 'business meeting' last night? Let me guess. She agreed to one, two, *three!* contract negotiations."

Andrew clears his throat but says nothing.

"What's her name?"

"Huh?"

"H e r   n a m e .   T h e   w o m a n   y o u conducted...business with last night."

"What does that have to do with anything?"

I stand, tired and ready to go home to my one woman. A quick stop at the jeweler's is in order, too. As I walk out of the hidden gym and into the expansive, bright room of Andrew's office, I call back.

"Enjoy your programmed life, little bro. When you're ready to join the rest of us, we'll be right here. Keeping it real. And now I'm going home to be real with Shannon."

"You mean you're going home to fuck her."

"Same thing."

CHAPTER FOUR

8:01 p.m. Shit. I'm the one who's late, so there's no need for a search party. My homing beacon is beeping like a fire alarm and as I fidget in the elevator, wondering why the hell I ever thought living on the top floor was a good idea, I hope she's home.

God damn New Zealand. The deal should be smooth sailing, and implementing this new line a breeze, but somewhere in the code, I know those sneaky developers added a cockblocking spell designed to keep me in a state of perpetual frustration because the name of the product we launched in twenty-three hotels and spas down under?

Blue Bell.

Which is so close to blue balls, which I have a raging case of, that I think all the sperm has backed up through my system and is poisoning my brain, turning me into a tinfoil hat conspiracy theorist. The developers in New Zealand are trying to drive me insane by preventing me from having sex.

There it is. I've completely lost it.

Shannon has a key to my place, and as I walk in the door I see candlelight. Flickering flame is to a man what Ben & Jerry's is to a woman.

A sign of a sure thing.

"Shannon?" I call out, following the disorganized scatter of lit candles in the living room. Shadows dance on the wall in my hallway, and I round the corner to my bedroom to find her, spread out on my bed, wearing garters, stockings, the red corset, and—

She's asleep.

That's okay. I can work with *asleep*.

I can't work with absent.

You'd be surprised how fast a man can undress when under the complete control of testicles so full they look like a case of mumps. I'm out of my clothes in seventeen seconds or so (who's counting?) and on the bed, my hands taking in her prone body. I'm allowed to touch. We have an unwritten rule. It goes something like this:

Touch Shannon.

It's a simple rule.

Her skin is so soft, my fingers scraping against the rolling contour of her inner thigh, from knee to heaven. The whorls of ridges on my fingertips feel like raw sandpaper against her porcelain flesh. My breathing slows, eyes adjusting to the dim light, taking in her body. How did I ever get so lucky?

From Toilet Girl to Mrs. McCormick in eighteen months.

Huh. I guess I count months sometimes, too.

The candlelight makes Shannon look ethereal, like an erotic painting, the red silk of her lingerie highlighting her pale skin. Her shapely hips, wide with the swell of abundance, are like magnets for my touch. The curve of her breasts beckons, begging for my palm. Climbing onto the bed, I prowl over her, enjoying the peace and beauty of this moment, suspended between the time we'll connect and these seconds before, when she's all mine to just watch. Observe.

Treasure.

Her feet slide up as she moves in slumber, her toenails painted the same color as her corset, her garters, her lips. For some reason, that attention to detail makes every shred of self-control wash off me like someone aimed a fire hose at me.

My mouth starts where it needs to be, with a taste between her thighs. My hands slip up between those legs and she sits up, gasping my name.

"Dec! You're home," she murmurs, her hand sinking into my hair, palm moving down to caress my cheek as I move up to kiss her. She awakens a little more and blinks hard. "And you're naked."

"You're observant."

"It's hard to miss *that*, even in the dim light." Thankfully, she doesn't just point. She *grasps*.

And that's it. She's under me and my mouth takes her, hard and hot, needing to sink into her and touch her depths so fully that we turn inside out. The taste of her mouth makes parts of me groan without sound, the sweet embrace of her thighs around my hips an invitation to enter at my own risk. And the risk?

Losing myself in her.

I'm an adventurous guy. I'll take the plunge.

The second I'm in her it's like coming home. A cliché, but true. Her fingers dance along my back, tight when she's clenching, loose and skimming my skin with her palms in between. I can read her body with my eyes closed. She's like sexual Braille. When her thighs start to quiver I know she's close. When her back arches, she wants my mouth on her nipple. That little hitched sigh? It means she's coming again. My name moaned when I'm between her legs?

That just urges me on. Makes me want to *give* her more.

"Declan," she whispers, the sound like a verbal orgasm. Our rhythm quickens and our kisses dissipate, the connection now focused on a different kind of energy, a sensual build that's nearing the summit. I love how her face changes when I'm in her, how she relaxes and turns inward, even as she's connected to me, infused by our mingled slickness. There's a scent we create when we're together that is singular, and it drives me crazy to find a hint of it on the sheets, on a pillow, to catch a whiff on a breeze through my bedroom in times when she's not here.

There won't be any more times when she's not here, though.

Not after I propose.

Her eyes are closed and she is the most ravishing, lovely creature I've ever touched, ever been with, ever loved. A man gets so few chances in life to find himself. We all live alone in these bodies, comforted by our own soul, driven by the mind to find meaning in the outside world. The heart drives us, too (and, of course, other muscles in the body with a single mission...).

She's fragile and strong, determined and insecure, gentle and iron-willed, and as my body fills with a groundswell of urgency, of pleasure at the feel of being in her, of watching her own release pour out of her because of me. I join her, raw and real, our mutual vulnerability the only thing that matters.

(And coming inside her, too. That matters. A lot.)

The room is so quiet. There's no wind today, and the windows are all closed in the bedroom, the candles generating a sandalwood scent and a hazy heat that charges the air with a kind of private grace. I'm worshipping at the altar of Shannon. My mouth has just taken my version of communion. And once I propose, I shall have no other goddesses before her.

She's my religion now.

"Mmmm," she says, pulling me to her for a kiss, that ripe mouth mine to pluck. "I needed that."

"You needed that? I was about to float off into the air like a weather balloon if I didn't—"

She curls into a ball, giggling, her pushed-up breasts jiggling like an unseen juggler's hands toss them into the air. Her nipples rub against the edge of the bustier and I'm entranced. Hypnotized. I could watch this for hours.

Who needs a fish tank for stress reduction? A red corset and a joke book for Shannon to read work just fine.

"All you ever think about is sex."

My stomach rumbles. My mouth stays shut, though, because she has a point.

"And food," she adds. "And work."

"And you."

"I think I'm filed under sex. Shannon is a subcategory under 'Places I like to stick things in.'"

"That would be Golf Courses."

"I'm your sexual golf course." She doesn't ask it as a question, but it hangs there, judgmental. I'm in the danger zone here. One wrong answer and it's into the penalty box for Declan.

"You don't have eighteen holes."

"No, I don't. I only have two."

"That you'll let me in," I mumble. That earns me a smack. I love it when she gets rough. My turn. I grab her and spin her on her belly, gleaming white ass so round and abundant. I'm about to give her a hot spank when—

Bzzzz.

"Whose phone is that?" we ask each other in unison.

My pants are buzzing. Damn it. I jump up and rifle through the pockets.

"Bet that's New Zealand," she sighs, turning over and sitting up, elbows on her knees.

Ah, the view. The view....

"McCormick," I snap into the phone.

"Hey, Declan!" says a voice so cheery it needs to be featured in a Pixar movie. "Greg here. Amanda told me you called and had a business issue to talk about? How's it going?"

I look at Shannon. She's making gestures that ask who it is. The problem is, I can't tell her. Greg is part of my whole proposal plan, and if she finds out, my perfect set-up goes down the drain.

I grab my wallet and toss it to her.

"I get paid for sex?" she asks with a twitchy smile.

"You should," I whisper. "Especially dressed like that."

She giggles and everything jiggles and I can't stop staring.

"But no. That's to order takeout. Thai?" She nods and scampers out of the room, that ass—oh, that breathtaking ass—departing as Greg's voice turns my arousal into a knot at the bottom of my stomach.

That growling sound isn't hunger anymore. It's frustration.

"Is Shannon there?" Greg asks, lowering his voice. "Did I—is this a bad time?" His voice slips into a register used only between men.

"She's here and she's fine. So listen, Greg, I need your help. It's about Shannon."

"I haven't called her in eight months!" he protests. "I don't ask her to do mystery shops for me ever since you played Santa and bailed me out! Carol's the one who got her to do that bookstore evaluation the other day. Not me!"

Bookstore evaluation? "What? No. It's not about that. It's about having Shannon do a mystery shop."

"You've lost me completely. I thought you banned me from having Shannon pick up mystery shops?"

"I did. This one is special."

"Okay. Like how?"

"I'm going to ask Shannon to marry me and I—"

"You're proposing! Congratulations! Couldn't happen to a nicer guy and gal. You know, Shannon's like a daughter to me, and you're like a—"

"Client," I say.

"Uh, yeah...client. A good client. A nice, big client I like very much professionally," he backpedals. "So how can I help my best client?"

"I don't want Marie to know I'm proposing. She'll stalk us. Bring a camera crew or something," I mutter, experiencing something close to a PTSD flashback as I stand here, naked, post-sex, talking about her.

"How can I help?"

"I want to completely surprise Shannon. Shock her. This proposal needs to come out of the blue, so I want you to have Carol ask her to do a high-end dinner evaluation at Le Portmanteau."

Greg lets out a deep, low whistle. "That place charges four figures for a single dinner." He goes silent. "Do they hire mystery shop companies? If so, I've never had a chance to bid on their contract."

Maybe I've underestimated Greg. I always considered him affable and a little clueless, but I'm hearing the hints of some quid pro quo here.

"You help me set this up for Shannon and I'll talk to their owner. See what I can do."

"That would be much appreciated!" Greg booms. "Let me get this straight. You want me to tell Carol to call Shannon and offer her the mystery shop. You know Carol and Amanda will slit my throat if I don't give them the chance to do this shop, right? They'll rip my balls off and stuff them up my—"

"I get the picture. How about this—I'll put in an order for three fake mystery shops. One for Carol, one for Amanda—"

Greg clears his throat. "Ah, Judy and I would—"

"Four. Make it four," I snap, hearing Shannon's footsteps coming down the hall.

"I put in the order for pad Thai and chicken satay! Enough for breakfast and lunch tomorrow, too!" she calls through the open doorway as she heads to the bathroom.

She's got my attention. An order that big can mean only one thing.

A sex binge.

The sound of the shower in the distance makes other parts of my body come to attention. I've got to get off the phone. Now. *Now now now.*

"Great. Take care of the details and bill me directly. This won't go through Anterdec. Make sure Shannon gets an evaluation form and instructions, an expense account...whatever it is you do. Make it look real. It has to be convincing." I start to get off the phone and add, "And this is confidential."

"Oh, my lips are zipped. No worries, Declan, and thank—"

I end the call and sprint for the bathroom.

There's just enough time for shower sex before the food arrives.

Shannon makes a great, wet appetizer.

Chapter Five

Four days before the proposal...

Going to Marie's yoga class is about as much fun as playing Mall Santa was last Christmas. With less pee and more pinching.

We have jock straps and cups to protect the jewels during athletic events, but there's no comparable product to protect your ass from the nimble fingers of a determined ninety year old named Agnes.

Shannon begs me to go. "Mom really feels bad about what happened with the, uh, cameras."

"Feels bad? Our first amateur sex tape was filmed by your mother. 'Feels bad' doesn't cut it."

Shannon's cute little nose scrunches up, her eyes narrowing as her eyebrows meet. "'First' sex tape? What do you mean by 'first'? That implies you intended to have sex tapes. More than one sex tape."

Damn it. Caught.

"I just thought someday...you know...."

"How about never. Someday is *never*. The camera adds ten pounds, and YouTube is forever. Plus, who wants to watch themselves having sex? Ew."

If the camera adds ten pounds to your tits or ass, go camera. I don't say that aloud, though, because I do not have a death wish. Scratch that one off my list of sexual fantasies. For now, at least.

How in the hell did we get from Marie barging in on us *in flagrante delicto* to my being the bad guy? "Look, I never taped us having sex, but your mother did," I argue.

"Technically, Agnes' grandson did," Shannon says primly. She really hates that I'm angry with Marie, and is doing the whole people-pleaser thing that she does when there's conflict. I think conflict is underrated. When two people clash, you learn more than you can ever find out when everyone's doing the fake passive-aggressive pretend game.

"It's hard to decide who to blame more, but I'm leaning on the side of Marie," I grumble. I'm driving my SUV out of the city and into the suburbs, toward Marie's yoga studio. Given that the proposal takes place soon, I should try to mend fences with my future mother-in-law. Give her a chance to apologize and all that, right?

"No one realized we'd be in a compromising position when Mom walked into my bedroom."

"Let's parse that sentence for a minute and find all the ways it's just plain wrong. Starting with 'Mom walked into my bedroom.' You're twenty-five years old and have a boyfriend. At a minimum your mother should knock."

"She's never needed to knock before."

"My point exactly."

"How did I just make *your* point?"

"Shannon, what kind of mother of a grown daughter doesn't stop for a second and wonder if

34

she's going to walk in on a private moment? For all she knew you were doing something indecent."

"I was!"

"Sex with me isn't indecent. It's private, and it's hot and sweaty and awesome..." What are we talking about here? I had a point, right? Now I'm just ready to skip yoga and go back to my apartment for another sex binge. We need to find a Thai place nearby...

"Then what would I be doing alone that's indecent?"

I frown. "You could be masturbating."

She makes a choking sound. "Wait. Having sex with you isn't indecent, but being caught...you know...is?"

"Right."

"Explain."

All this talk about having sex and Shannon taking care of things herself is making my mental picture gallery and video archive turn into one big sexfest. I slip up. I err.

I tell the truth.

"Because that would be a waste."

The temperature in the car drops a good ten degrees.

"A waste?"

"Right. You have me now. You don't need to...you know..."

The look on her face makes this tiny little voice in the back of my head scream *Do over! Do over! Abandon ship! Abandon ship!*

"Let's go back to the word 'indecent.'"

Uh, oh.

Bzzzz.

Saved by the phone. I'd rather be screamed at in Balinese than hear whatever's about to come out of Shannon's mouth.

It's a text from Marie.

> *Yoga cancelled due to water leak in studio. You kids have a fun afternoon. Don't do anything I wouldn't do!*

That list is so small.

"Your mom just canceled yoga," I explain as I get into the left lane to pull a U-turn and head back into the city. "Water leak in the building." Broken pipes are so underrated.

Shannon's still upset, but pivots. "Text her back and let's offer to meet for lunch."

"Do we have to?" I can't keep the gruffness out of my voice. That Resting Asshole Face quality applies to my voice, too. I have a bad case of Resting Asshole Baritone, apparently.

"You hate my mother," she says out of the blue, bursting into tears.

Oh, shit. Just what you want your future fiancée to say four days before you're about to pop the question.

"I don't hate her." Diplomacy bubbles up at the perfect time. "I just need more space than you do when it comes to Marie."

"What's *that* supposed to mean?" Shannon's eyes are red and puffy already. Something in my chest feels like I'm being stabbed. "It's not like I wanted her to come in like we were filming an episode of Sons of Anarchy!"

"There was a motorcycle in the room?" I'm lost now. Then again, there *could* have been a motorcycle in the room for all I cared. When I'm having sex with Shannon, the rest of the world just fades away.

"I meant your naked, sculpted ass on video." I've seen the episode of Sons of Anarchy that she's talking about. I sit up a little straighter knowing she thinks my ass is that muscled.

Wait.

How did she see my ass from that angle?

I pull over into a parking lot and slam the SUV into Park.

Her eyes widen, a creeping flush of red starting in her neck and moving up. Turns out I'm not the only one who's caught.

"You *saw* the video?" The only way Shannon could know something like that was if she viewed it.

"Have *you*?" Her chin juts up in defiance. Didn't expect that question.

It's a standoff. We stare at each other with narrowed eyes, like characters in a really bad spaghetti western, the kind my grandfather used to love to watch on Saturday afternoons.

"How did you see it?" we ask in unison.

Stare.

God, she's sexy when she's filled with righteous indignation *and* lying to me.

"You told me you got the camera from those boys and destroyed every version of the video," Shannon says slowly, pulling back from me in the front seat and giving me a look meant to convey that she was being cagey and viewed me as a pervert, all while running through a visual loop of my naked ass in her mind.

I can see my own ass in her eyes. She's transparent like that.

"I did. But the kid without the camera was using his phone to tape everything. Said they were taught in media class that they should always have back up."

"Great. College freshmen who actually *listen* to their professors," Shannon mumbles, crossing her arms over her chest in fury. "Just our luck." She frowns. "You deleted it off his phone?"

"No," I say, patting my pants pocket. "I bought the phone from him." Nice phone, too. Better than mine, which makes me realize I've become a dinosaur in the tech world. Need to hire an eighteen-year-old geek to keep me supplied with the latest gadgets.

"You bought his *active* phone on the spot? Phone number and all? He just *gave* it to you?"

"I didn't really give him a choice."

She goes silent.

"How did *you* see the video?" I ask.

"Agnes' grandson had a flash drive in the camera. So there was a copy. He gave it to Mom and she gave it to me."

I smash my fist into the steering wheel and she jumps, terrified. I don't *do* violence. Hitting things is a sign of weakness, a symbol of the inability to use words and power to get what you want.

Which is why I hit the steering wheel.

Marie has made me resort to pounding the car dashboard like the frustrated oaf that I've become.

"Did your mother watch it?"

"No. She swears."

"You're sure she didn't tweet it to Jessica? Make some popcorn and invite Agnes over? Offer a still for the side of a promotional vehicle?"

"You're taking out your anger on the wrong person," she replies with a coolness I've never noticed in her before. Looks like Shannon's been getting some lessons in Resting Bitchface.

I wince at the thought. And her words...

"I'm sorry. You're right." I turn the car on and put the car in Drive, but her hand stops me, covering mine on the gear shaft.

Knowing I'll see eyes filled with reproach, I look at her slowly, dragging my gaze.

What I get, instead, is a kind of ragged lust.

"What did you think about the, uh, video?" she asks breathing roughly through her nose, her face carefully neutral.

"It was mercifully short."

"That's all?"

"And hot." The video lasts about six seconds, a clear view of my always-pinchable ass and Shannon's gorgeous legs, quite a bit of fevered movement, and then the screaming starts.

First the cameraman (who knew a guy could hit that octave?), then Marie, followed by what I think is Chuckles' laughter. I don't know. I've never heard a cat laugh before. But if cats can laugh, that's definitely the sound.

"Oh, yes." The top of her tongue pokes out of her mouth and suddenly, I'm breathing hard, too. See? This is why I thought maybe, some day, we'd make our own little personal porno.

But I never thought my future mother-in-law would beat me to the punch.

"All the copies are gone, though," I assure her as that hand moves from the car's gearshift to *my* gearshift. I go from neutral to fourth gear in three seconds.

Shannon's right.

All guys really do think about is sex.

"Let's get out of here," I murmur as I reach over and kiss her neck.

"Where?"

I pause and inhale through my teeth, the hiss the sound of relief as she gives me a contrite look. Neither of us was wrong, but neither of us was right.

(But she's *more* wrong, of course).

"How about we go back to an old haunt," I say, turning toward the road that leads to the trail we were on nearly eighteen months ago when she almost turned my penis into a pincushion.

"Where?"

"You'll see."

"Not the gas station where you insisted we try to have a quickie?" I can't tell if she's making an offer or being sarcastic.

"I made a joke. Once," I growl.

The rest of the drive we're silent, though she reaches over to hold my hand, her lips remaining in a neutral, straight line, eyes hooded. The Incident is one thing, but the relationship between me and Marie is another. Shannon wants everyone to be one big, happy family. I get it. I do. But I come from a family environment where everything warm and fuzzy ended the day something warm and fuzzy stung my mother and killed her.

My concept of a big, happy family is one created from wistful memories, snippets of movies, and the occasional invitation to someone's parents' private island for Thanksgiving.

"Oh!" Shannon perks up as I make a right turn into the gravel-coated parking lot for the state park. She smiles. Something in me loosens.

You might think I'm out of my mind for bringing an anaphylactic bee sting patient to a park in Massachusetts in August, and you'd be right, except that Shannon—unlike my vampire brother CEO—has decided that she will not restrict her life in any way because of her allergy. She goes outside, she hikes, she all-but beekeeps a set of apiaries in her zest to live a "normal" life.

Frankly, she missed the boat on a "normal" life with a mother like hers and falling in love with a billionaire's son, but I like to humor her.

We climb out of my SUV and before we can shut the doors a bee floats past my face, lazy and stupid.

"God damn it," I bark, pointing at the .025 ounces of death with wings.

Shannon shrugs.

I open my door. "Get in. We'll go somewhere else." What the hell was I thinking? Adrenaline streaks through me like I've been injected with it.

"See?" She jangles her purse and reaches in, pulling out two EpiPens. "I have two. One for me, and one for your penis."

I should be in a conference room right now. Million dollar contracts should be presented before me, arrayed like a fan, with entire divisions of companies hanging in the balance, waiting for my decision. That kind of power is what I handle best. Finding weakness, shoring up strength, making money, making more money—that's what Declan McCormick does. It's in my blood. It's who I am. Power, influence, and authority are my trifecta.

Out here, in nature, where a single insect could steal the most precious being in my life away from me, though, none of that matters.

Not one shred of power can stop Shannon from dying because of a single random god damn drop of poison on a bee's ass.

And I can't do anything about that. The fucking bee wins.

Sure, she has those EpiPens in her hand, and we can race to a hospital again. I could cloister her and make her stay inside eight months out of the year, living in constant fear like my brother.

Or I could walk away. Break it off. I have every right. This hits too close. My mother died and Shannon has the same, exact vulnerability and it's killing me that no matter how many millions I have in the bank, no matter how many businesses rely on my decisions for sustenance, no matter how many people I control, I have to place my heart in Shannon's hands and trust that everything will be fine. My life with her stretches out into a captivating eternity, and if she doesn't walk the entire journey with me because of a bee appendage no bigger than a splinter, I—

I don't know.

I have no other option.

She walks around the SUV, takes the keys out of my open hand, beeps the locks and starts walking down the trail. She's a hundred feet or so ahead of me before I choose to take a step toward her, willing myself to stop scanning the air for bees like a Special Ops dude on a mission.

"My penis," I call out to her, "doesn't swell up when it gets bitten."

Just then, two hikers come out from around an enormous oak tree. I pretend not to notice them as I catch up to Shannon. They're snickering. That's okay. I'm accustomed to public ridicule being par for the course when it comes to being with Shannon. Remember #HotSanta?

"Your penis," Shannon says under her breath as we continue the walk up the hill toward the meadow where we first began to make love and she almost died. Those two phrases really shouldn't be in the same sentence. Ever.

"My penis what?" It responds to sound and is listening intently. She leaves those two words hanging.

She pauses and reaches into her back pocket, pulling out her phone. It's buzzing. I groan.

She reads the screen. "Carol. Can I come and watch her kids for an hour while she does a quick mystery shop?"

I groan louder.

"Or," Shannon asks pointedly, "she says I could do the shop for her instead." Shannon's eyelashes flutter and she looks at me with mischief. "It's a dropped sex toy shop. The mystery shopper who was supposed to do it was a no show. Carol has no choice. In fact," she adds, trying to butter me up with a coquettish look, "I was doing nine dropped mystery shops the morning I met you."

I narrow my eyes and try to stare her down.

She doesn't budge.

Damn. That used to work.

"You and Greg promised me you'd stop doing shops," I say, knowing I'm full of it, because any day now Greg's going to beg her to do the fake restaurant shop for me.

"You're right," she says, tapping away on the screen.

"What are you typing?" I can see the edge of the field where we can walk to privacy. Shannon grabbed the backpack with our blanket in it as she got out of the SUV, and I have a condom in my wallet....

"I just let her know we're on our way to pick up Tyler and Jeffrey to take them out for ice cream while Carol does the mystery shop."

I look at the field.

I look at Shannon.

The Field of Dreams in one direction.

The Children of the Corn in the other.

My shoulders slump and I start walking back to the SUV. "Fine," I say as she lifts an imaginary chain attached to a body part and leads me off to babysit.

CHAPTER SIX

"When are you going to be my uncle?" Jeffrey demands as we walk through the front door to Carol's apartment.

I look at him. He can't stop grinning and giggling. Wait a minute. Something's off.

"Marie!" I say in Resting Asshole Baritone. "I know you're here somewhere! How much did you pay him to ask me that?"

Shannon pulls a one dollar bill out of her pocket and stage whispers as she hands it to him. "Nice try."

"Grandma paid me five buckth. You're cheap, Thannon." She gives him a huge hug in spite of the insult. I give him a high five not for the uncle comment, but because I can admire a budding entrepreneur. Jeffrey may be my investment banker someday if he keeps this up.

And my nephew, too.

"You need a hug," Tyler announces from the hallway, the corners of his mouth turned down in sadness.

I bend down and open my arms.

He screeches, "I will not! I will not!" Carol comes rushing to my rescue as Tyler offers himself to Shannon for an embrace.

"Let me guess," I say slowly, puzzling through the intricacies of Tyler's language disorder. "He was really saying 'I need a hug' and he was saying it to Shannon.'"

"Good! You're becoming increasingly fluent in Tylerish!" Carol chirps. She looks so much like a young Marie that I worry about Dad meeting her one day.

Which would be, most likely, at our wedding rehearsal dinner.

Wedding.

Proposal.

"He's actually fluent in Russian. Remember?" Shannon winks at me.

"Chuckles smells like a pickled egg shoved inside a rotting gerbil," I say in Russian.

Carol freezes and slowly looks at Shannon. Chuckles walks out of the room in a huff. He loves me. I know he'll forgive me, but I'll check my shoes before I slip them on when I'm here.

"You get the hot billionaire and he speaks Russian? All I got was a tattoo'd musician Internet Marketer wannabe with an entitlement complex who left me in credit card debt hell."

Shannon shrugs.

"He has two brothers!" Marie calls out from the back room. "Isn't that perfect? You have two sisters, Shannon, and Declan has two brothers."

"If you and my dad married, Shannon and I would be stepsiblings," I say.

Marie turns pale as Jason walks into the room. Do these parents ever spend time in their own homes?

"What's this about Marie marrying your father?" Jason asks, the corner of his mouth twitching. At first, I think he's trying not to smile, but then I see the clenched jaw. The tight fists. He's angry.

"Declan was making a joke. It's not funny," Shannon says. I, on the contrary, think the look on Marie's face is hilarious.

"Why are we babysitting when Marie and Jason are here to help out?"

"I have to go to work, and Marie's scheduled for the mystery shop with Carol," Jason explains. "Otherwise I'd invite you over to my place for a brew." He's wearing a paint-streaked t-shirt, jeans, and flip-flops. At his house, he doesn't even bother with the flip flops most of the time. Jason's as casual as my father is formal. They're a study in contrasts.

Marie looks at me with a pained expression in those bright blue eyes. "Declan? A word in private?"

My hands are in my pants pockets, fingers touching the phone I paid $700 to get out of that kid's hands in the moment. I offered $300 but he countered with a grand. Negotiating with my naked front covered by a Strawberry Shortcake pillow from Shannon's childhood left me in a woefully weak bargaining position.

"Private?" I say quietly to her. "Is there such a thing as privacy with you?"

The barb makes her flinch. Jason's watching us carefully, and I see his shoulders tense. I'm treading on very unstable ground here, but I don't give a shit.

Then again, I do. I should. With a pending proposal and a commitment to be a member of this family for the rest of my natural life, the part of me that defaults to sarcastic zingers might need to pull

47

back. In the McCormick family, fluency in Sarcasmish is a requirement.

While Shannon's family is full of one-liners and witty jokes, there's no razor edge to the words. Feelings are easily hurt. People here actually have real emotional reactions to painful words.

There's no wall like the one I was taught to build, brick by brick.

Sting by sting.

Marie nods toward a small bedroom to the right. It must be Carol's, and I realize that in a year and a half of dating Shannon I've never been in this room before. The walls are covered with giant maps, beautiful, textured, nuanced maps of each continent. No country names—no words at all. Just a visual, the oceans made of a very pale seawater green, the continents a muted rainbow of varying shades of beige, green and brown.

I'm staring, and Marie's watching me, a proud smile on her face. "Carol's a mixed-media artist in her spare time."

"She has two kids and a job and has spare time?" I ask. "According to Shannon, Carol doesn't have time to shower most days."

Marie laughs, but it's a restrained sound. Marie isn't a restrained person, so it's telling. "Carol majored in art in college until her ex convinced her to drop out so she could make enough money to support them during his 'career' as an Internet Marketer."

"Ah. Todd," I say. It's hard to keep the acid out of my voice. Jeffrey worshipped his father and begged Santa—me, in disguise—to bring his dad home for Christmas last year. Despite every call, text, and email outreach possible by Carol, no dice. The guy didn't even bother to send a Christmas card to his own kids.

Loser.

"Carol was always my wild child," Marie says with a loving sigh. "She's had a hard life."

Who hasn't?

"What is this?" I ask, changing the subject, touching the odd pebbles that appear to be meticulously glued together to make the maps.

"Coffee."

"Coffee?"

"Coffee beans," Marie elaborates. "Carol buys green coffee beans in bulk. Roasts them different colors. Then she makes her art."

Terry would have a field day with this. He's the creative one in the family and while Dad hates it, he's—

"I'm sorry about your ass," Marie blurts out.

Here we go.

"My ass is fine. It's my pride that's hurt. More than that, though, it's Shannon. That was one hell of an invasion, Marie, and I can't have you doing that anymore."

Marie hangs her head in the closest thing to shame she's capable of feeling. Her hair doesn't move with her at all. The woman must use the equivalent of a can of SuperGlue to keep it in place.

"I know. We just have a pretty free kind of family —"

"You have no boundaries. Shannon does."

Marie's face flashes with anger as she looks at me. "I've apologized for barging in on you having sex while a camera crew filmed me. I've tried to make amends. You're a hard man, Declan."

I smile without showing teeth. "I take that as a compliment."

She shakes her head slowly. Sadly. "You need to learn how to forgive and move on."

It dawns on me that her sadness isn't about her rudeness in barging in on us, but is directed toward me. As if *I'm* the sad one. Being the object of her pity isn't high on my list of goals.

"I don't need to do anything, Marie. I've done nothing wrong."

She pales. "You don't...I don't..." Her frown deepens and oh, no—are those *tears*?

I see where Shannon gets it.

"Declan," she says with a tiny sob in her voice. "Everyone makes mistakes. Everyone."

My perfectly reasonable, one hundred percent unassailable, totally understandable and perfectly justified righteous indignation is being threatened by the salt water in her eyes.

This is unfair.

"And in our family, when someone makes a mistake, they go to the person they hurt and they apologize. Sincerely and truly. And then, because we love each other, the person accepts. They forgive. They move on."

Now there's a fairy tale, right? Because who does *that* in real life?

She's watching me carefully, without guile.

Oh, shit.

She's serious. She really believes that this is how people work. Maybe in schlocky sitcoms. But I've been alive long enough to know that forgiveness is just a catch phrase that people with character disorders use against the weak.

At least, that's what Dad always says.

"You want me to forgive you," I say, clarifying.

"I won't demand it, but it would be nice. You have a way of behaving that feels like the knife is being twisted a bit," she answers.

"Maybe I'm not ready to forgive." The words are out before I realize they're all wrong. I'm conceding, aren't I? Just mentioning the idea that I *would* forgive *if* I were ready shows a willingness to negotiate, and everyone knows the first rule of negotiations is never, ever to speak first.

(The second rule is not to do it naked after your mother-in-law's barged in on you having sex).

She beams a smile of happiness that makes me feel like Tony Robbins is going to chew me out the next time I see him at a conference.

Marie just won.

Flinging her arms around me in an embrace I don't reciprocate, she squeezes me twice, gives me a kiss on the cheek, and flees out the front door with a purse slung over her shoulder.

What the hell just happened?

How did I go from being aggrieved party to the one who was chided for not forgiving?

The look on my face must betray what's going on inside, because Jason comes over to me and slings an arm around my shoulder.

"You've just been Marie'd."

51

"What?"

"Marie'd. She got you. Welcome to the family."

As that sinks in, I realize I haven't even proposed yet and I'm being manipulated by people I'm not legally obligated to interact with.

The kids run into the kitchen past me and Jason.

"You want a cheese stick," Tyler declares, opening the refrigerator door.

"We're going out for ice cream, honey," Shannon explains. "You want some?"

"Tyler wants ice cream!" Tyler says. Tyler's like the Bob Dole of little kids, always talking about himself in third person. It's amusing. Very gradually, he's replacing his name with 'I', and as he begins to talk normally Carol's thrilled. I think it's pretty cool that he has a mind that works differently. Those are the people you really want to hang out with.

Tyler will develop something big some day, the future equivalent of the Internet, or the cell phone, or he'll head Anonymous. I want to stay on Tyler's good side.

"Say, 'I want some ice cream, please,'" Carol says in a patient tone.

"I want some ice cream, please," Tyler repeats perfectly. He's nearly seven now, and while he's still way behind kids his age, he's really come a long way. Marie, Jason and Carol have acted as a unit, receiving training and support from speech therapists and teachers at Tyler's school, and it shows. I admire that. The big, happy family really kicks in with the Jacobys when one of them needs help.

Maybe there's something to this forgiveness bullshit.

Shannon offers a palm to Tyler. "High five!"

Tyler turns to me, ignoring her, and gives me a closed fist. "High zero!" he declares.

We fist bump.

That's the closest he comes to saying *When are you going to be my uncle?*

Soon, kid. Soon.

I hope.

"Ice cream, huh?" I murmur in Shannon's ear, giving her a kiss on the earlobe. "You're my favorite flavor."

She smiles and blushes, entwining her fingers in mine as we hold hands and herd the two excited boys outside for the walk down the street to their favorite ice cream stand. Carol's already pulling out of the driveway with Marie. I can see Jason climbing in his car and he waves, a friendly smile plastered across his face.

We walk on the sidewalk, a couple with a stroller walking past us, going in the opposite direction. Shannon peeks in the stroller's top and makes a sound of gushy surprise, a little "Oh!" that indicates her ovaries are ready to hijack my sperm and put them in a half-nelson, pinning them to her uterine wall.

First things first. I still need to propose. But watching Jeffrey and Tyler make their ambling way down the road, the four city blocks like their own personal obstacle course, makes me think about kids. We want them. Shannon's made it clear that she needs to have her career in order before she'll consider having any, but I think she's already softening.

Having kids will slow us down. First, I want to spend a few years taking her all over the world to cross items off my bucket list. We've never been to Paris, and Shannon has talked about wanting to see Machu Pichu. Can't do that easily with a baby strapped to your front in one of those contraptions.

I could give a laundry list of all the various experiences we both want before we have kids, but instead I'll just focus on the fact that Shannon is suddenly holding a screaming Tyler, whose nose has turned into Mt. Vesuvius, complete with red blood spurting all over Shannon's shoulder and chest.

"What happened?" I bend down to check it out.

"Tyler tripped," Jeffrey explains. Simple enough.

Shannon's rocking him back and forth while he screams, "Wipe it off! Wipe it off!" as he smashes his palm into his bleeding nose. Every two seconds he does the same loop: wipe, look at it, scream "Wipe it off," and then repeat.

"Hey, buddy. Hang on. Are you hurt?" I ask.

"NOT! NOT HURT!" Tyler likes to deny anything negative. Spill his juice? No, he didn't. Get his feelings hurt? No, he didn't. Bloody his nose? No, he didn't. He's great at denying reality like that. He could be the Fox News correspondent on climate change.

Shannon hands me her purse. "Can you find tissues in there?" Her purse is a bottomless pit of practical items you might need once in your life, seven tampons, two EpiPens, a few lipsticks, countless receipts, and one lottery ticket.

Finally, I find tissues and hand them off. "Lottery ticket?" I ask, incredulous.

She begins to gently wipe Tyler's nose. "It can't hurt to try," she says in a sing-songy voice.

"I'm a billionaire," I say slowly.

"Only on paper. I know how that goes. Steve was a 'millionaire'." She actually uses finger quotes. True, her ex-boyfriend, Steve, was a pompous windbag with the financial management skills of one of the real housewives of Beverly Hills. That prejudice does not apply to me.

" I am a *real* millionaire," I remind her. "And damn close to being a billionaire. You need a lottery ticket like Taylor Swift needs Spotify. "

Jeffrey overhears this. "You are? I'm gonna have a rich uncle? That ith tho cool! Do you have a helicopter?"

"Yes."

"And a grey tie?"

Huh?

"Because Mom is always reading this book at home about a billionaire who wearth a grey tie. It's on the cover of the book and everything."

Oh, God.

"He has fifty tieth! Fifty! Why would a man need so many tieth?" Jeffrey's lisp becomes more pronounced as he gets excited.

"Um..."

"Fifty! Fifty!" Tyler repeats, laughing. He has so much blood on his face he looks like he's an extra in the movie *Saw 27*.

"Is there another tissue in my purse?" Shannon asks. I look. Nope.

She frowns, and I see the problem. As we both ignore Jeffrey's innocent questions about Carol's mommy porn, I realize Tyler looks like we just smashed his face against a cement wall. He can't go out in public like this.

"You have a key to Carol's apartment?" I ask, certain of the answer. Of course she does. Her family has no boundaries. They probably all share toothbrushes in a pinch.

She shakes her head sadly. "No."

"No?"

"Mom does but I don't."

"Shit."

"Shit," repeats Tyler, perfectly. He, unlike his older brother, does not have a lisp.

It's a warm August day, and I'm dressed for the canceled yoga class. Black polyester shirt, black shorts. Grabbing the hem of my shirt, I whip it over my head.

"While I love the view, what in God's name are you doing?" Shannon whispers.

"Shirtless men aren't exactly a rarity in August in Massachusetts," I whisper back.

As if I'm approaching a spooked cat (because I pretty much am), I crouch down and lean on one knee. Tyler's face is buried in Shannon's chest. Her pale pink t-shirt now looks like a bad tie-dye job.

"Tyler? It's okay. I just need to wipe the blood off your face."

"You will NOT!" His eyes are wide and panicked, and I realize my error immediately. I might not know much about kids in general, but after a year and a half of spending holidays and occasional babysitting nights with Tyler and Jeffrey, I have a good sense of what to do.

Plus, I was a six-year-old boy once. There's really only one way to proceed.

"Did I say blood?" I ask in an exaggerated way, like an actor on a kid's television show. "You don't have blood on your face, do you?"

"No blood," Tyler says with suspicion. At least he's stopped screaming.

"Of course you don't have *blood* on your face," I say, holding my bunched-up black shirt near his face. "But," I whisper, pulling him in like I have a secret to share, "you do have *poop* on your face."

"Poopy?" Tyler asks. Shannon gives me a *Really?* look with an eye roll that must hurt.

Jeffrey starts giggling and comes closer to where the poop talk is. If you ever run out of topics to talk about with boys under the age of, oh, thirty-five, just talk about poop. It's the universal language of immature males.

Fine. *All* males.

"Do you want poop on your face?" I ask Tyler.

"I don't see poop," Jeffrey says, frowning. "All I see is blood."

Panic returns to Tyler's eyes.

"It's not blood," Shannon says to Jeffrey, pulling him to her and whispering furiously in his ear. His face changes to an *I get it now* look.

"Tyler," Jeffrey says excitedly, "you are covered in poop! It's like you, like you..." He's frowning, trying to come up with something wild and crazy.

He succeeds.

"It's like you were eating poop!" Tyler and Jeffrey descend into giggles as Tyler says "We don't eat poop!" eleven thousand times in a row.

Shannon gives me a disgusted look. I shrug. The kid's not screaming anymore, is he? In fact, he's howling with laughter. Still covered in blood, which makes him look like a mini Dexter, but—

I got this.

I totally got this whole Dad thing down.

You just talk about poop.

"I'll let it go this time," Shannon says as she snags my shirt from my hand and Tyler lets her wipe away the "poop" from his face, "but I don't want to hear you talk about poop again."

"But—"

"Poop comes from butts," Jeffrey says, like it's the best joke ever.

Jeffrey, Tyler, and I fall apart laughing, but Tyler lets her clean his face. Shannon has to lick my shirt here and there and wipe hard, but by the time she's done he looks mostly okay, if a little pink.

She hands me my shirt. I unball it and put it on.

"You're going to wear that?" Her nose crinkles in disgust.

"What? It's got warrior paint on it."

"It has poop on it!" Jeffrey declares as we get closer to the ice cream stand. No line today, which is a surprise for an August day.

"Poop shirt!" Tyler screams. Shannon walks ahead of us and puts in our standard order.

"Okay, guys, let's stop with the poop talk. Auntie Shannon doesn't like it," I say as I pull them into a huddle. Tyler doesn't seem to understand what I'm saying, and Jeffrey certainly does, his face crestfallen.

I take them over to the jungle gym and they play for a few minutes, Tyler begging for a push on the swing, Jeffrey climbing up a rope and ramp. Shannon appears with a tray of ice cream cups and we sit at a picnic table.

It's like we're normal. Like we're a family. I can imagine having two boys like Jeffrey and Tyler and taking them out for a fun afternoon like this (minus the nosebleed).

Shannon distributes the ice cream and we dig in, muted by sweet cream and sprinkles on top.

Jeffrey starts giggling uncontrollably. Shannon and I look at him, perplexed. He points to Tyler.

Tyler's chocolate ice cream is all over his face. The kid managed to get it in his hair and along the ridge of one ear.

Jeffrey is squealing with painful howls of laughter, and can manage only one, single word:

"Poop."

I grind my jaw trying not to laugh, and Tyler repeats everything Jeffrey says.

"Poopy face," Jeffrey sputters. Tyler repeats him twelve thousand times.

"This is all your fault," Shannon hisses at me. "I do not ever want to hear you make poop the topic of conversation again."

"What? It's not my fault!" I put my hands up defensively. "It got Tyler to calm down."

"It's disgusting and you know better than to get two little boys started on poop jokes."

"Poop is hilarious."

"Poop is not a conversation topic!"

"I beg to differ."

"No more poop talk. I am done with poop talk. I never, ever want to hear about poop again, as long as

I live. I don't talk about poop, and you don't need to, either. Are we understood?"

She'll regret those words.

CHAPTER SEVEN

Three days before the proposal...

"That," Dad says as he hands the ring back to me and picks up his half-empty highball glass, "is a gorgeous ring. Still is after all these years. Your mother wore it well. Cost me a small fortune back then." His pipe burns, half-abandoned, in a small ashtray. Smoking's not allowed in Boston, but James McCormick insists the rules don't apply to him when he's the owner of the building.

His hand is steady as he lifts the glass to his mouth but he drinks it all in one long gulp.

And signals to the bartender for another.

We're in the lounge at The Fort. Dad likes to pop in on his favorite property from time to time. There's a soft spot in my heart for this place, too. After all, you don't watch your future wife drop-kick a vibrator down fourteen floors into Boston traffic every day now, do you?

Ah, memories.

"I always thought Terry would be the first to marry," he adds, looking mournfully at his empty glass. "He's the oldest."

"Terry is about as likely to marry as you are to date a fifty year old, Dad." Terry's a musician who travels all over the world and is just starting to dip his toe into investing in really fringe web concepts for music. Not only does Terry lack a permanent address or a permanent woman, he doesn't even own a car. The guy is minimalism personified.

His biggest commitment is his international cell phone plan.

Dad laughs, the sound dismissive. "What you're telling me is don't hold my breath on a wedding for Terry."

I give him a tight smile. Dad shakes his head slowly, eyes on the ring I'm still holding in my palm. It feels hot, as if the metal were pulsating from within.

"I suppose if neither of your brothers is anywhere close to marriage I might as well give it to you," he says in a gruff voice.

"Congratulations, Declan," I say with great affect. "Let me shake your hand and give you best wishes for your pending wedding." I clap a hard hand on his shoulder. "There's your script, Dad."

He snorts. "Shannon's perfectly fine in all the right ways except one, Son. I'm not going to bullshit you on that. You know I think you're in for a world of hurt if you choose a woman with the same medical condition as your mother."

"And I don't give a sh -- " He perks up as a cocktail waitress with an upside-down, heart-shaped backside that makes Nicki Minaj's ass look like a flattened balloon appears with Scotch in hand. We both watch her walk away. It's so...mesmerizing.

"You can't tap that once you give Shannon that ring," Dad says with a chuckle, grasping the drink like it's a lifeline.

"Don't want to tap that."

Dad sucks down his drink. That's his third since I arrived an hour ago.

"Good. Because if I get enough liquid courage in me, I think I'll give it a try."

I do a double-take. "If she's thirty I'll be surprised."

"If she's thirty I'll be disappointed." Dad shoots me a leer that's meant to be shared, a sexual conspirator's smile. I keep my face neutral on purpose. Shannon made a troubling comment a long time ago about my dad dating women her age, and it's stuck. She was right. They call him The Silver Wolf. Not fox. There's a difference.

Dad's the stereotype of the uber-rich old dude sticking it in anything born after the fall of the Berlin Wall.

And he's *proud* of it.

Shannon's theory is a pretty wretched one: after my mom died, Dad couldn't deal with his emotions and funneled them into rage at me. He's angry with me for not saving mom when she and Andrew were stung and we had only one EpiPen. I was the person who literally had to choose which one lived. Dad can't process his grief for Mom without sublimating it into anger.

And I'm the convenient target.

I think Shannon's been watching a little too much Dr. Phil.

Dad's dealt with those feelings with overachieving pushes toward Andrew to become CEO, and abandonment of Terry, who's always been the black sheep of the family.

Dipping his wick in women under thirty became a way of keeping his emotional distance, too.

I think the truth is much simpler:

He's just a sexist asshole.

Or just an asshole. Period.

But he's my father, and my boss, so I roll with it. It's none of my business who he chooses to bed. Until he declares he's marrying again and the will's being changed, his private life is none of my business.

My sex life, on the other hand, is about to go public.

Again.

Because once you propose to a woman, you're pretty much declaring to the world your intention to fuck her. A lot.

Impregnate her, even.

The thought of Shannon pregnant, belly swollen, body glowing with new life makes me lose focus. A warm feeling of protectiveness and gratitude fills me. Either that, or my second scotch is kicking in. No, it's not alcohol. It's a feeling only Shannon can bring out in me.

"You've got it all planned out? The perfect proposal?" Dad asks with a smile. He's sincere. No sarcasm. That's a surprise. Maybe it's the alcohol.

"I do." Those two words have new meaning.

"And you're not telling anyone a damn thing."

"No." Dad juts his chin up and waves to someone in the distance. Andrew walks into the lounge like he owns the place. Technically, Dad does, but who's keeping track?

Technically, Dad is...

The server looks up and gives Andrew a suggestive smile. Dad scowls.

"You know her?" Dad asks Andrew, competition flaring in his eyes. Dad's got that whole Most Interesting Man in the World schtick going for him, with the greying hair, attractive features, and the billionaire mystique, but Andrew's got youth on his side. Some women want George Clooney.

Others want Jamie Dornan.

And Dad hates that.

"I've known her. Biblically," Andrew says in an undertone.

Dad just sighs. Being the old lion must be tough. Even Clooney just got married.

Andrew turns to me and taps my arm. "Speaking of knowing people biblically, you're about to propose. Got the ring?"

"Yep." Andrew doesn't know Dad gave me *Mom's* ring. I'm going to keep it that way until it's on Shannon's finger.

Competition works in a lot of different ways in our family.

"And the proposal's planned?" The server brings our drinks over, obviously memorizing Andrew's preference. Dad gives her a dazzling smile and she returns a polite one. *Give it up, Dad.*

"Yep," I say, impatient now. The testosterone level at the table has reached Titanic drowning levels. I need a door to hang on to. Talking about proposing to my sweet, warm, loving girlfriend while drowning in the toxic wasteland of my brother and dad's masculine oneupmanship feels like I am stuck with one foot each on two tectonic plates that are shifting. Fast.

And my balls are about to take the kinetic hit.

Andrew cocks an eyebrow and looks exactly like pictures of Dad thirty years ago. "Why the secrecy?"

"He doesn't want Marie to know when and where," Dad says with a wistful tone. Among the stranger aspects of my relationship with Shannon I have to include this fact: Dad and Marie dated many years ago, before he met my mom. Which means nothing in the grand scheme of things, but it's still a little disturbing.

The rehearsal dinner is going to be so much fun.

Andrew snorts. "Smart man," he says to me. "I can understand why. What's her deal? She have a head injury in her past?"

"No. That's just how Marie is."

"You must love Shannon very much to accept that kind of mother-in-law," Andrew adds with a smirk.

Dad's looking ill at ease. The fact that he and Marie have a past is a vulnerability he'd rather not possess.

A sudden wave of nerves hits me. I don't *do* nervous, so it's doubly disturbing. Andrew swallows half his drink and gives me a speculative look.

"What? Spit it out?"

"You'll be my best man?" Those words: Best Man. Holy shit. This is real. Really real. Not that getting the ring, having it secretly sized for Shannon, calling Greg and arranging a fake mystery shop, and calling Le Portmanteau to have the perfect proposal setting in place wasn't real.

But those words. Best and Man. Best Man.

I'm getting married.

Married.

Is the room spinning suddenly? Perhaps Boston is experiencing an earthquake. Maybe someone slipped a roofie in my drink. Because one minute I'm upright and the next I'm on the ground, head between my knees, with Dad mumbling, "Jesus Christ" far above me.

I've died and gone to hell, haven't I?

"Dude, you are going to be the worst groom ever if you're passing out at the simple thought of proposing," Andrew says from five miles out into space. "We'll need an oxygen mask and a defibrillator to get you through the ceremony." Andrew helps pull me up on my chair. "And yes, of course I'll be your best man." He smirks. "Take that, Terry."

See? Competitive.

"You don't have to marry her if you don't want to," Dad grouses.

That makes me sit up more.

"What? No." I snap, still feeling a bit off. "Of course I want to marry her. What the hell's wrong with you, Dad?" I spit out.

"I, unlike you, am upright and conscious."

"Two more drinks and that won't be true, Dad."

He just shrugs, drains his glass, and signals the server for another round. He's a walking self-fulfilling prophecy with a bank account big enough to make himself immune to consequences.

Suddenly, I can't be here. Can't keep doing this. Watching Dad be a lech, talking with Andrew about my future wedding like it's a cage, I just...I'm done. I need someone who can listen to me without judgment. Without sarcasm.

Without looking at everything in the room that has a vagina like it's eye candy.

I stand up, head clear now. "Gotta go."

"Where?" Dad asks, but he's not really paying attention. His eyes are using x-ray vision to see through the server's skirt.

"An appointment with someone very important."

CHAPTER EIGHT

The drive from Dad's hotel out into the suburbs is frustrating, filled with a traffic jam caused by the flood of college students going back to school. Car after car overloaded with suitcases, pillows, household goods and lamps clutters the route I normally take.

Finally, the off-ramp clears and I am on the side road, winding through a small town center to get to my destination. At a red light, a car to my right honks, a light tap that indicates someone's trying to get your attention. I look.

It's Marie.

She waves wildly, a big smile on her face. It's infectious. I smile back and wave, wondering if this means I really have forgiven her. What's she doing in this town? It's not one of her normal haunts.

A flurry of hard honks follows. I look up and realize my light's turned green. Gunning the engine, I take off, feeling a bit foolish, but the smile lingers.

The long, twisting country road outside of Concord always fills me with a sense of foreboding. A sick chunk of concrete settles into my stomach, and it's not because the New Zealand project looks like it's one of my few failures.

It's because I remember driving down this very road eleven years ago to bury my mother. Tree-lined and lush with the bloom of late August, the memorial park could be a town center with wide walking paths, save for the gravestones sprinkled everywhere. My throat tightens as I maneuver the SUV through the iron gates to the sprawling cemetery where my mother's family is buried.

I park and walk to a small hill, an enormous beech tree covering half of it, the tree like an elephant's foot, only ten times greater in diameter. Mom's stone is under the shade of the tree, though not directly under it.

Grey marble. A simple message. Her name, her birth and death dates, and an inscription:

Loving wife to James, mother to Terrance, Declan and Andrew

More than ten years ago I rode in a black limousine behind an oversized black hearse that carried my mother's body. Dad had delayed the funeral until Andrew was out of the hospital, and Terry had come home from college.

You couldn't talk to Dad. His secretary fielded questions from the three of us. An impenetrable fortress closed around our father, and he was all surface, no depths. At the time, he seemed so shallow, so insincere, like he was playing the part of the wealthy, grieving widower and we were just props. The three boys. Elena's beloved sons.

If anyone got us through the emotional nightmare of mom's death, the credit really does go to Dad's secretary.

Grace.

Mom and Dad were only children, so we had no passel of aunts and uncles to descend and help.

Mom's father was dead, and her mother was in a nursing home back near Buffalo, New York. Dad had broken off all contact with his own parents years ago for reasons he still won't share. About five years back I learned they were dead.

That big, happy family wasn't us. Never had been. Mom was the glue.

When you lose the thing that keeps you together, everything falls apart.

Grace's arms are the ones I remember reaching around me as I stood for hours after the burial, refusing to get in the limo, incurring the hissed wrath of Dad but not giving a shit. Andrew and Terry had complied with Dad's order to get in the fucking car *or else*.

I chose *or else*.

No one except Dad cared that I stayed. They all went back in a long line of more than one hundred cars under police escort, headed for the Farmington Country Club for the sedate, tasteful gathering where appetizers would be served and wine and spirits would flow and we'd all have some closure.

That was Dad's word.

Closure.

I'd stood staring at the mounded dirt over the hole in the world where someone had dropped my mom. Her body wasn't just in there. My future was, too. Leaving her wasn't an option. Once I walked away, once I got into that black machine and drove off and left her like everyone else, it sealed the fate of truth for me.

I'd killed her.

Dad had said that to me the day we'd gone to the hospital, the day he learned her throat had closed, swollen so far that no amount of love or drugs could pry it open. Andrew was hanging on in another room but Mom was dead.

Dead.

All we have are memories of the dead. No more kisses. No more arguments. No more forgiveness.

You can't forgive a corpse.

Or, in Dad's case, a son.

A wave of shame covers my body, a feeling I haven't experienced in eleven years. Suddenly, Marie seems wise. Maybe she has a point. When you love someone, part of that loving involves digging deep inside yourself to a truth that is only yours. Whatever hurt and pain and grief resides inside you, that truth needs to be reached. Pulled out. Held up to the light of day and reconciled with the love you feel for someone who you feel did you wrong.

I was barely eighteen. In an impossible Catch-22. Saving my brother meant losing my mom. Saving my mom meant losing my brother and defying her panicked plea.

No way out.

Things fall apart. The centre cannot hold. Mere anarchy is loosed upon the world....

Mom helped me deconstruct that Yeats poem right before she died. It's about WWI and the terrible ravage of a war that changed all the rules of brutality. All the rules of what was expected when things fall apart.

The ceremony of innocence is drowned...

How could Dad blame me? How could he not? I suppose I understand and yet I don't. My gut twists every time I think about those wretched moments when she and Andrew were stung and the weight of the world was placed in my hands. Every time Dad makes a snide comment.

Every time a bee floats past Shannon.

Am I crazy to marry a woman who could die the same way my other did? I must be. A little. Two EpiPens can't hold back the danger and the risk. My wealth means I can buy all the EpiPens in the world and sprinkle them liberally in every corner of every place where Shannon and our future children will be.

And it still might not be enough.

Love doesn't care about randomness. Love embodies it, in fact. Embraces it. Knows that the random is the vehicle for spreading joy.

And pain.

So much pain.

Surely some revelation is at hand...

My father focused on the pain, never the joy. I followed in his footsteps. That serendipitous moment in the bagel store. Finding Shannon with her hand down the toilet. Having her walk into that meeting at my office and taking her to dinner...

Falling for her.

Loving her. Loving her so much I'll risk letting my heart fall apart for the profound honor of her willingness to be mine. And to love me back.

The joy of being with her outweighs the potential pain. It's a gamble of the heart that I'll just have to take, hoping the odds are on my side.

"Things fall apart. The centre cannot hold. Mere anarchy is loosed upon the world," I say aloud to my mom.

God, I love Shannon so fucking much I'm standing here in front of a gravestone muttering Yeats to a dead woman.

I've brought Shannon here before to "introduce" her and Mom, and we visited on Mom's birthday and her death day. "Death Day" is one of the most macabre terms ever invented, but there isn't a better term. Death Day it is. Shannon's watched me cry here, seen me rage here, and we've also enjoyed a glass of Mom's favorite wine while sitting on the quilt my grandmother knitted for Mom when she was pregnant with Terry.

Mom's had a reasonable chance, to the extent that one can while dead, to form an opinion of Shannon.

It's time to hear what the woman who owns the ring thinks.

Am I little crazy to be doing this? That's a rhetorical question, right? Because no. Fuck anyone who thinks so. When you decide to propose to someone you talk to your parents, their parents, your siblings and friends and your secretary and the mailman and the barista where you get your macchiatos, right?

Why wouldn't I have a lengthy conversation with a gravestone, too?

Loving wife to James, mother to Terrance, Declan and Andrew

How does a life sum up in one sentence carved in stone? She was blonde sweetness and light. Firm disciplinarian and kisser of boo boos. She taught us how to "read" an original painting, and why white space is important in art and life. Elena McCormick found a gentle peace in handwriting letters on fine stationery. She loved to walk in creeks barefoot and jump into the ocean before sunrise, freezing and laughing as Dad watched from the balcony of the beach house, cup of coffee in hand, shaking his head at her antics.

She was the sigh as she kissed me goodnight when I was little. The brush of hair against my cheek when she forced a hug from my teenage loner self. The scent of expensive perfume as she walked through the room on her way to a black tie fundraising dinner with Dad. The gleeful eyes as I brought my first girlfriend home to meet her.

The only person in the world who told me that being Declan was my job. That finding out who I am was more important than being who everyone else wanted me to be.

Mom would have really, *really* loved Shannon. I came here a few weeks after I met Shannon and told the story of how we met. If she were alive, Mom would have been horrified, then laughed so hard she'd have waved her hands in front of her eyes, begging for mercy because her mascara was running.

She'd have insisted I bring Shannon home to meet her, and the two would have hit it off. Mom may have been Boston blue blood, but she was authentic, too. Polished and refined, but genuine.

Shannon is anything *but* polished and refined. In fact, she's the very definition of rough around the edges. But she's real and authentic, raw and *mine*—and I am so fucking angry that Mom never got the chance to see how happy we are.

Life really, really isn't fair.

The only thing I can think to do right now is punch the tree. Eleven years ago, after all the cars were gone, the last red taillights rounding the corner to exit the cemetery, that's exactly what I did.

Punched the tree until my knuckles bled so much they dyed the tree bark. Grace had stopped me, hugged me, and just held me, sobbing.

My hand must have been in better shape when I was eighteen, because one sickening thud and I'm all punched out, with bones that are screaming at me in glorious pain.

"Declan?" says a woman's voice, older and smoother than Shannon's. A light breeze tickles the leaves on the trees and I choke up, spooked.

"Mom?" I say, jumping like a ghost just appeared, my voice cracking like I'm going through puberty.

Her gravestone remains in place and I think I'm losing it. Hearing voices in a cemetery must be a form of mental illness, even if grief can make you want to believe they're not really gone.

I've had eleven years, though. I know damn well she's gone. All too well. Is this what unraveling feels like? Maybe I need to bag the whole proposal, because I don't want to saddle Shannon with a husband who's losing it.

Husband. I'm going to be her *husband*. The word hits me like a stone between the eyes and I look at Mom's grave. Dad was her husband. Mom was the love of his life.

And she *died*.

All because of me.

"No, honey. It's Marie." I whip around and there she is, standing back, hands clasped in front of her and tentative. She reminds me of how Grace looked after everyone left the burial, just waiting in the wings until I was ready to leave, holding my bloody knuckles, arms around me as I stumbled to her car.

"Marie?" There are a wide variety of people I would expect to run into at my mother's gravestone, but Marie doesn't make the shortlist.

"I saw you in town and texted to see if you wanted to have coffee. Then I followed you."

I clear my throat. She throws her hands up, palms facing me.

"I know! I know! Boundaries," she says with a sad smile, looking at Mom's gravestone. "I was just worried that someone had died."

I raise one eyebrow. "We *are* in a cemetery."

"I meant someone new had died. That something had gone wrong." Her eyebrows meet in that pitying, older way that Grace has perfected. Marie has been taking lessons from someone, or else it's a look that comes with menopause.

"No. No one new has died. Just my mom." I look sadly at the gravestone.

Things fall apart.

So do people.

"Oh, Declan. It's never 'just' when it comes to losing your mother. And you were so young when it happened."

My mouth tightens in what is supposed to be a bitter smile but just feels like anger. "It's been eleven years. I'm over it."

"You never get over losing a parent."

My eyes fill up with what I assume is an allergic reaction to something in this damn memorial park, because I don't cry. Men don't cry. That's a McCormick family rule, too. We drink, we fuck, we excel, we dominate, but we don't cry.

Marie moves her neck, looking up at me to catch my eye. Would my mom have those crow's feet, too? She didn't eleven years ago, but Marie has the advantage of living these eleven years. Of aging. Of mothering her children and being alive. The years wear a person down and leave an imprint on their face, their skin, their body, their heart.

But the alternative is so much worse.

"Declan? Why are you here?"

"Can't a—" My throat is clogged and I try again. Damn allergies. Apparently, I'm developing them suddenly here. "Can't a guy visit his dead mom once in a while without needing a reason?"

She nods. "Fair enough." We stand in quiet, a lawn mower starting in the distance. The buzzing sounds just enough like a wasp that I flinch.

Marie's eyes are alert and clever, watching me. But she doesn't say a word.

"You look like James, but there's something about you that must come from your mother," she finally says. "Andrew is the spitting image of your father. I've never met your oldest brother. But you..." She smiles kindly and reaches up to brush a piece of hair out of my eyes. The gesture is unnerving. Motherly.

"It's the hair, ironically," I explain, pulling back a few inches so she can't touch me.

Marie's eyes flit between my mom's grave and me. She opens her mouth, lips parting, then snaps them shut. Once, twice, three times. Whatever she's struggling to say, she's going through monumental effort to do it, and I'm really not looking forward to it.

"Tell me about that day," she says gently.

My eyes close and my shoulders drop. I don't have to ask her what she means. The band of steel that snaps shut like a trap door when this subject comes up isn't there. Shannon pried it open shortly after we got together for good and I told her the whole story.

She's the only person, other than medical authorities, who has ever heard it. Dad didn't want to know. Even Andrew has never asked. He knows what *he* remembers, but not what I experienced after he passed out.

And now, Marie.

"There's not much to tell. We went to one of Andrew's soccer games. It was May, the day before my senior prom. He was a sophomore and I was a senior and Mom was filled with the craziness of planning my graduation party. She was lecturing me on how to treat my date because prom is every girl's dream, and Andrew was teasing me about making sure I got a nice hotel room so I could deflower her," I say, the words slow, my mouth filled with cotton and regret.

Marie makes a small noise of encouragement.

I can't help but grin at the memory. "Yeah. Mom loved that. Smacked him upside the head and told him he was being vulgar."

I sigh. The memory isn't just a series of images in my head, retrieved to repeat and tell. It's like they're living in my mind, like I can smell the freshly-cut grass around the soccer fields, hear the ref blowing the whistle, the shrill sound cutting through my thoughts.

"Mom wanted to go for a walk while Andrew was between games. She loved the trails in the park. There was this creek that we played in as kids. Lots of rocks and little pools. The perfect place to bring rowdy little boys for an afternoon." My voice hitches on the last word. I imagine me and Shannon taking Jeffrey and Tyler there and make a mental note to mention it to her.

I think it might be good to revisit there on a happy note with little boys who can play and throw rocks and get muddy.

I've never been back.

"And we were walking near the water when a swarm flew by. It just—pure randomness. You ever see a wasp or bee swarm?"

Marie shakes her head.

"It's marvelous." I can hear the wonder in my own voice. "Frightening and powerful. Hypnotic. At first you have no idea what it is. The damn thing looked like a ball of darkness in the sky, moving impossibly through space. My eyes kept trying to pattern match and turn it into birds. And then, as it passed overhead, we realized what it was."

"Mom shouted and ducked. Andrew just stood there, stunned, like me. And then he screamed, a high-pitched sound like a little kid. Again." I'm reliving it now, eyes stuck on the word *loving* on Mom's gravestone.

"Mom made a funny noise of pain, a muted sound. I remember shoving Andrew down to the ground, with Mom, and he jerked, grabbing his leg. By the time the damn wasps were gone he'd been stung at least three times—the doctors weren't sure about a fourth sting—and Mom twice."

"Oh, God," Marie says quietly. I can't bear to look at her. She'll have tears in her eyes. And if I'm going to tell the story, I just can't look at her.

"Mom told me to stay calm. We knew she had a bad allergy and I knew she had an EpiPen in her purse. Andrew was screaming. No one was anywhere near—we were at least a half mile from the soccer fields, though you could hear the loudspeaker announcements from a distance. Mom handed me her purse. I knew what she meant."

I can remember the warm touch of her fingers as we exchanged the bag. Her manicured nails, a pearly pink. I can't say that part aloud. It's mine. Private.

"'EpiPen,' she croaked, her breathing labored already. I could see the two stings on her elbow as she pulled her shirt up."

"Two?' I remember shouting."

"'Andrew'," she rasped, crawling over to him. And then I realized, as I found the EpiPen in her purse, that she wasn't the only one struggling to breathe."

Marie is crying softly now. I can hear her. She comes up to me and places a hand on my forearm. I don't move, but my eyes start to leak.

Damn new allergies.

"'Where are you stung'? I asked him, and Andrew pointed to his calf. Two stings, then one on his neck. He sounded like he was having a horrible asthma attack."

Gravel on the road behind us crunches as a landscaper's truck drives through, equipment loaded on the back. The sound of the lawnmower is gone.

Good.

It sounds a little like a swarm.

"Mom pointed to Andrew, then the EpiPen, then back to him. 'Inject him,' she said, sounding like she was choking." I finally look at Marie. "And I froze."

"Anyone would, Declan. Anyone. And you were just a boy."

I squeeze my eyes tight and go on, watching it behind my closed lids. "'No,' I said. 'You need it, Mom.' She just shook her head, hard, and tried to grab the damn EpiPen from my hands. Andrew was passing out. Mom's lips were turning blue and she grabbed my face so hard, looked in my eyes and said, 'Do it.'"

Marie squeezes my arm.

"So I did. I opened the pen and shoved the needle as hard as I could in Andrew's thigh, and then I got up and ran as fast as I could to the soccer fields. Could barely breathe, but said enough to get all the people who had cell phones to call 911."

"You did everything right," Marie says, patting my hand.

"Did I? Did I really, Marie? Because my mom is dead. Dead. I didn't do anything right that day."

"What else do you think you could have done, Declan?" she asks, digging through her purse to hand me a tissue.

"What's that for?" I ask.

She points to the front of my shirt. It's wet.

"Oh." I wipe my eyes with my palms.

"You did everything right. Andrew lived. No one could have ever guessed he was allergic, too. And your mom asked you to save him and you did."

"But I couldn't save them both!" I'm shouting at her. She is crying but not scared. That's because I'm not angry at her. I'm angry at a world where I couldn't save them both.

The same world I have to live in, day in and day out.

"Why did Mom make me inject Andrew? Why did I listen to her? If I'd injected her, maybe Andrew would have been fine. And then—"

Marie grabs my arm, hard this time, with a yank that isn't at all compassionate. It jolts me and makes me look down at her.

"You listen to me," she says in a hard voice. A mother's voice, the kind moms use when they are disabusing you of an errant notion. Her finger comes out and she shoves it in my face, making a point. "Your mother did what any mother would do. That's what being a parent *is*, Declan. When you are dying and your child—your baby—is dying right in front of you and only one of you can live, you beg that your

83

child lives. Because no parent could ever bear to live in a world where there was a choice and they chose themselves."

"But—"

"No, Declan. No buts. I don't care what you've been told or who has told it to you, and that includes your father. You did nothing wrong that day. It was not your fault. No one can control everything. No one. The world just keeps proving that over and over again. You did nothing wrong."

If I squeeze my fisted hands any harder my fingers will snap off.

"Declan. *Declan*," she insists. "If you had injected your mother and Andrew had died, that would have been so much worse for her. Do you understand? She needed you to save her baby. You did exactly what she wanted most in that moment. You took a terrible situation and made the best of it. You were heroic. You were your mother's hero. You didn't have a true choice. She made it for you. That was part of her gift to you. She loved you and Andrew so much that she took the choice away."

My shoulders start to shake and I fall to the ground, head between my knees, eyes fixated on that carved word.

loving

"Come here, honey. It's okay. Come here," she says, giving me no choice in whether I get a hug or not, dropping to the ground next to me and wrapping her arms around me as I curl into a ball. Marie smells like sandalwood and vanilla, like makeup and laundry detergent, and she is warm. Soft. Motherly.

The sobs come out in embarrassing ways and I fight it, but I miss my mom. I miss her. If I could stop the world and turn back time, I'd go back and kill those wasps before they stung Andrew and Mom. I'd pack two EpiPens. I'd not go outside at all with them.

I'd do anything to have my mother alive right now.

No business deal, no hard-core negotiation tactics, no lavish spending can bring her back.

Neither can closing off my heart and running away from the love of my life.

And her crazyass family.

"I can't be your mother for you, Declan," Marie says, smoothing my hair as I wipe my nose on my t-shirt hem and compose myself, feeling like a weak, oversharing jackass. "If you let me, though, I can be *like* a mother."

"But you are *crazy*, Marie." I'm not smiling as I say it because I am not kidding.

She smiles and says, "Not clinically."

That makes me laugh. We stand and brush off our clothes. A breeze rustles my hair. The sky is blue and wide, without a single cloud in it. Rare for a Massachusetts day.

"I just love too much, Declan." She tips her head to the right and gives me a look I don't think anyone but my Mom and Grace have ever given me. "And whether you like it or not, you're one of my kids. You didn't come out of my vag—"

I hold up a palm. "I get it. I don't need the anatomy lesson."

"But you're part of Shannon's heart, and that means you're part of our family. Which means you're in a web of people who love each other so much they do crazy things because they feel so intensely," she adds.

"And because you're crazy."

Marie links her arm in mine and looks pointedly at Mom's grave. "Elena, you raised a fine young man. Thank you. Whenever he decides to pop the question and officially become my son-in-law, I'll take over for you and continue the raising."

I give her the side eye. "I'm twenty-nine years old, Marie. No one needs to *raise* me."

"You think you're done, don't you?" she scoffs. "I'm fifty-three—er...in my forties—and I still need my mom sometimes." Marie's mother died of a heart attack a few years ago. Not a bee sting, Shannon assured me.

"We all do, don't we?" A sniff or two, a short sigh, and we both seem to have composed ourselves. I feel raw. Exposed. Like maybe I've given in to my emotions too much. Dad calls displays of emotion "melodrama," and even though I understand he has the emotional development of a borderline sociopath, I can't shake the feeling that this is all a little too much.

I've completely underestimated and misunderstood Marie, though. She's great in her own weird way. Maybe Shannon's right about her mom. Maybe I've misjudged her.

I look over and Marie's watching my hands as I brush off my bottom.

"You do have a fine ass, though."

Sigh.

"Marie," I growl. "Boundaries. Would you say that to your own son?"

"Maybe. I tell Shannon I'd kill for her boobs."

Resting Asshole Face: Engaged.

"Okay, okay! Sheesh! Is it my fault that *some* people can't take a compliment?" she declares as we walk back to where our respective vehicles are parked.

It's going to be a very long marriage, isn't it?

Chapter Nine

Two days before the proposal...

We're at work, talking in the hallway. I'm between conference calls, and it's been the kind of day that started at 4:30am with a crisis in Singapore and is going to end at 2 a.m. with a crisis in Dublin. I can feel it.

Meanwhile, a crisis is brewing right here, right now, between me and my beloved.

There's this look Shannon gets on her face when she has to tell me something she's not sure I'm going to like hearing. Her face tightens a bit, and she looks pained. Concerned.

Matronly.

A lot like Grace the other day when she was in my office, grilling me about my pending proposal. Minus the chicken soup and crappy advice.

"Just say it," I might as well cut to the chase. When I'm at a negotiation I find the direct path is easiest. Insecurity is a wasted emotion. Wondering, worrying—all of that is just inefficient. An emotional drain. A horrible use of resources better spent elsewhere.

(See why I would make a good CEO? Tell that to my dad.)

Shannon's shoulders drop and she starts playing with the ends of her hair, curling them up, almost chewing on them. It's cute when she's restless like this, but it's ominous, too. Whatever she's about to say is going to suck.

"Um, so, Greg called today."

Oh. *That*. As far as I know, Greg's kept the fake mystery shop conceit a secret, as planned.

"And?" I can play along. She thinks I'm going to be mad that she agreed to help Greg out in a pinch with a mystery shop. I keep my grin in check.

"And there's this one job..."

"We agreed," I say slowly, like I'm talking to a disobedient child, "that you wouldn't do any more mystery shops. I played Santa for an entire suburban mall in exchange. I was *hashtagged*." I unbutton my suit jacket and lean against the wall, ignoring the phone vibrating in my breast pocket.

"#HotSanta was pretty cool," she says with a tone of cheeriness that reminds me what a good elf she was.

And then there was that costume. Ho, ho, holy smokes.

"#HotSanta existed for an hour and a half, but the odor of pee on my legs from terrified kids is branded in my scarred psyche for a lifetime."

She pretends to punch my arm. "C'mon. This is a mystery shop at Le Portmanteau."

I pretend to be impressed. "Really?"

"Full meal. We have to order a bottle of wine. And the shop fee is $300!"

I multiply that by four. Greg's sharper than I thought. Affording it is no problem, and I'd spend ten times that on flowers to fill her apartment with roses if I thought it would make an impression.

Somewhere deep inside, though, I feel like I can hear Greg laughing at me.

Laughing from the finest table at Le Portmanteau.

Focus. I need to focus. Shannon's looking at me with excitement. "This is exactly the kind of shop secret shoppers dream of landing."

"You're an assistant director of marketing now. Those dreams should be dead." My words echo in the room. Shannon's right. I do have Resting Asshole Baritone.

She raises her eyebrows at me, blinking those big, brown eyes. "Someone woke up on the grumpy side of the bed."

"*Someone* woke up at 4:30 a.m. with a screaming tech director from Singapore complaining about a web issues, and then *someone else* got up later and came to work without having sex with *someone.*"

She crinkles her nose and huddles with me. "Please don't talk about sex with me in public at the office. You know we've talked about this."

Shannon's so cute when she's protecting her professionalism. Yes, I know that makes me sound like an asshole. No, I don't care. She's smart, funny, great with clients and she's helped push marketing conversion rates through the roof for explorative online campaigns in emerging social media.

I can admire all that and talk about her like she's a piece of meat.

"Okay. I won't," I concede. But not really. "How about we find a nice supply closet somewhere and talk about sex in private here at work?"

Her deep sigh is tinged with frustration.

So's mine, but I think for different reasons.

A commotion down the hall, at Dad's office door, catches our attention. We both turn to look and hear a woman say, "No, I do not have an appointment, but this is important."

A flash of a blonde helmet of hair on top of a flowing lilac dress shoots into Dad's office.

Shannon and I turn to each other. "Was that—?" we ask in unison.

"No," we say at the same time, shaking our heads.

"Can't be," Shannon insists, but she's giving me a skeptical look that manages to have a strong pleading element to it. Like she's begging me to say that is absolutely, positively *not* her mother making a scene in my father's office.

"She wouldn't dare come here and crash Dad's office," I add.

Shannon cocks one eyebrow.

"Right?" I ask. Funny how now I've got a pleading tone, too.

"I can't believe you would—" shouts a woman's voice.

"You have some nerve coming in here—" bellows my dad.

Slam! A door shuts and Dad's administrative assistant, Becky, comes running out of the office. She sees me with Shannon and trots down the hallway as fast as one can trot in five inch heels.

Dad picks his admins for their sex appeal. Not their practical qualities.

"Some crazy woman just charged into the office claiming she's an old friend of James' and she needs to see him," Becky says, breathless. Those baby blues are big and wide, with an impossible amount of white around them, framed by black eyelashes so long she could sweep floors with them. Becky's got a nipped waist a man can span with his hands and boobs so fake and big they might as well be airline neck pillows.

"Call security, then," I say casually, trying to decide the best approach. Why would Marie, of all people, storm my dad's office? It's not as if she knows about the proposal.

And even if she did, what does Dad have to do with it?

"Old friend?" Shannon asks, grabbing Becky's forearm. "Did she say anything else?"

"It was really weird. Something about how she picked the right guy and how dare he treat Declan like—"

I am not wearing five inch heels. I sprint into Dad's outer office and fling open the inner sanctum, Shannon right behind me.

"MOM?" Shannon shouts.

Marie is leaning across Dad's enormous desk, hands planted on stacks of papers, her face inches from his. She is saying something in a low voice and Dad is paying angry attention to every word. I can't hear her because of the shuffling sounds Shannon and Becky are making behind me, but as Becky recedes back to her desk and Shannon starts hyperventilating, I can parse most of it out.

"...and I can't believe you would blame Declan for Elena's death like that."

Oh, fuck. I knew yesterday was one big, big oversharing mistake. Marie just proved it. Shannon looks at me as I rub my mouth with my hand, calculating how to salvage this giant mess. Dad doesn't do feelings, and Marie is one big walking heart covered in perfume and new-agey clothing.

This is not going to end well.

"What is she talking about, Dec?" Shannon whispers in my ear, her hand between my shoulder blades on my back. The solidity of that palm grounds me, helps me to react from a place of logic and centeredness, rather than grabbing Marie around the waist and flinging her down an empty elevator shaft.

Shannon and I have been so busy with our respective schedules that I haven't even had the chance to tell her about my run-in with Marie at the cemetery yesterday. Even if we had time, I'm not sure I'm ready to talk about it.

Guess I'd better get ready now.

"Your mom followed me to my mom's gravesite yesterday."

Shannon's eyes bug out. "What?" Dad and Marie are arguing in tight, gritted-teeth sentences, their heated discussion a backdrop for my emotional evisceration.

Dad is going to kill me.

"I went there to visit my mom, and Marie happened to see me at a stoplight. Waved. I went to the cemetery and was talking to my mom and Marie appeared."

"She stalked you?"

I'm not going to throw Marie under the emotional bus, no matter how tempting. "No, nothing like that. She was worried about me."

Dad starts pounding the top of a stack of papers with his middle knuckle. Shannon casts a nervous glance at them. So far, Marie seems to be holding her own and no one's ordered us out.

"And storming James' office today has something to do with that?"

A sick sort of snicker I can't control comes out. "I don't know. It's Marie, after all. She's kind of crazy."

"You know I hate when you say that."

My palm out, I make a grand, sweeping gesture toward our arguing parents. "Case in point."

Her lips purse but Shannon says nothing.

I win.

"...how I handle my relationship with my sons is absolutely none of your business! I haven't seen you in—thirty years?—and you think you can tell me how to parent?" Dad's shouting now. It's the sound of my childhood, the scary, terrifying voice of someone who is supposed to be authoritative and wise losing it.

"You clearly need lessons on basic human decency if you've spent a decade alienating your son and shaming him for something no mortal human could ever fix! He couldn't save them both, for God's sake. Get over it before you lose Declan as well as your wife!" Marie shouts back, chest heaving and face livid.

Shannon's mouth drops open with shock.

Mine, too.

My soon-to-be fiancée leans over to me and hisses, "What *did* you and Mom talk about yesterday?"

That sound you hear next is me, being catapulted emotionally back in time, the thump of my body. I'm eighteen now, suddenly. Eighteen and wearing a suit, running an international division of a Fortune 500 company. Eighteen and watching my dad get a righteous comeuppance from a woman who told me yesterday that while she can't replace my mom—and would never want to—she thinks of me as one of her own right now.

"Declan?" Shannon pulls me aside and we're hidden behind a large bookcase, the kind that's filled with burgundy leather-covered classics and law books, statutes and other Very Important Writings in tomes meant to convey seriousness. Power. Privilege.

"Honey?" Shannon asks, stoking my cheek. I'm frozen, back to that day as I watch Marie take my dad down verbally.

Without warning I grab Shannon and kiss her, hard and furious, the blood rushing through my ears and crescendoing, like a set of stringed instruments all warming up at the same time, in harmony. The low rumbling invades my mind and now my arms pull Shannon against me, hands in her hair, my tongue tasting her.

She pulls away, lipstick smeared, eyes blazing. "We are at work!" she rasps. "Whatever's going on inside you," she adds, softening but still furious, "I understand you're—""

I kiss her again.

The door opens and in storms Jason.

"Oh, my God, is that my *father*?" she hisses, wiggling out of my arms. I can't think. Can't strategize. Can't calculate or plan for whatever contingencies keep coming. Her family is like a giant game of human Whack-a-Mole. No matter how many times you think you've made them disappear, they just keep popping up.

It's easier to just kiss her.

"I knew it," Jason says. Shannon's kissing me back now. We're completely hidden behind the bookcase, and if Marie and Dad realize we're still in the room, they don't give any sign of it.

I pull away and look on the shelves.

"What are you doing?" Shannon asks, mouth red and boobs bouncing with heavy panting.

"Looking for whisky. We're going to need it." No decanters. No flasks. Just a very dusty set of Samuel Pepys first edition Harvard Classics. Not getting inebriated on that any time soon.

"Now, this is just ridiculous," Dad announces, walking around the front of his desk in a confrontational manner. "Who in the hell are you?" he asks Jason.

"They've never met?" I whisper to Shannon, who really looks like she could use that whisky.

"My mom...my dad...yelling at the owner of the company where I work..." she mutters in short phrases.

And your future father-in-law, I think.

"Jason Jacoby." Jason glares at Marie, who is combing over him from head to toe. Jason's dressed in a suit and tie, clean shaven and has a nice, new haircut. He looks like any other businessman in his fifties.

Except I've never seen Jason dressed in anything other than jeans.

"I'm the husband of the woman you're fucking," Jason declares, eyes right on my dad.

And Shannon's eyes roll back. She falls against me in a dead faint, slumping to the ground, her skirt riding up her thighs and her hair mashing into the Persian carpet next to the bookcase. Great. I'm about to propose to Scarlett O'Hara. Fiddle-dee-dee.

I'm pinned to a small table next to us and gaping at her. I'd faint, too, if my father accused my boss of fucking my mother.

This is one of those moments where you decide which kind of man you are.

One who cowers behind a bookcase in your father's office while your future father-in-law accuses him of fucking your future mother-in-law?

Or a grown-up who goes out there and tries to mediate.

That's right. I grab a pillow off the leather chair nearby and place it on my lap, gently moving Shannon's head onto it and settle in.

This could be a while.

"I had no idea Becky was married!" Dad roars.

Oh.

"Becky? Who the hell is Becky? I'm talking about Marie!" Jason shouts, matching dad's volume.

Shannon's eyelids flutter, her soft eyebrows bending down in consternation as she comes to. I've never seen her faint before, and while I know stress can do that to a person, having her drop like a sack of potatoes in the middle of this fiasco just feels like a giant joke.

Let's take inventory for a second here:

1. Marie has invaded our workplace.

2. She's lecturing my dad for being a jerk after my mom died.

3. Dad just revealed he's porking his admin, which is against company policy (Shut up. I am *not* a hypocrite. Shannon is not my direct report.).

4. Jason has barged in and accused my dad of *schtupping* his wife. The wife who dated my dad long before my oldest brother, Terry, was a twinkle in anyone's eyes.

5. Shannon fainted, with her face in my lap and not in the fun kind of way.

6. Everyone's screaming at each other and all I want to do is put my mother's ring on Shannon's lovely finger and make sweet love to my fiancée.

There's the recap.

Not one bit of that makes sense except for the last part, and as Shannon sits up and looks wildly around the room, her hands cold and shaking, we hear:

"Out! Both of you! Before I call security!"

That's *Marie* shouting. Shannon and I jump to our feet and race around the bookcase to find Jason and my dad on the ground in their suits, wrestling.

"Jesus Christ," I mutter.

"She's mine!" Jason grunts as he gets Dad into a messy wrestling move. I take it Jason learned how to fight in the streets in south Boston. While we three McCormick boys learned fencing and boxing at Milton Academy from instructors who competed in the Olympics, Dad was a street kid, too. A Southie street kid.

Two Southie guys on a thirty-year hiatus from a brawl? This could get interesting. If nothing else, they both have middle-age paunches to work around, and while I know Dad has gym-toned arms, Jason's been doing his own yard work for the last three decades.

And they seem to have checked their civility in the same place where their common sense is hiding.

"You—" The rest of the filth that comes out of Dad -- a stream of invective aimed solely at Jason, Jason's mother, Jason's genitals, and stretches back about six generations -- is a product of Dad's Irish-Scottish heritage. Mostly his Scottish heritage, because Scots don't forget anything when it comes to insults.

It's in the DNA.

Marie starts screaming, "I don't know what's gotten into Jason!" while Shannon looks at me in horror.

"Do something!" Shannon shouts at me.

What the hell am *I* supposed to do? I'm not exactly trained in techniques for breaking up a fight between your future father-in-law and your dad. Besides, there's more to this fight than meets the eye. I could stop them. I have the power (and could probably take them both in a fist fight. Scratch probably. *Definitely*).

Letting people show themselves to the world, though, gives me more power than shouting and making them stop. There are many ways to take charge. To dominate. To be a leader.

Sometimes stepping back and observing is more effective than taking action.

Shaking her head and muttering something about useless billionaires, Shannon grabs a water spritzer that Becky uses to spray the spider plants in Dad's office, marches over to the four hundred pounds of aged meat wriggling and grunting on the floor, and sprays them.

Over and over, like dogs.

"My suit!" Dad shouts, holding up his palms. "Don't ruin this suit! It costs more than your annual bonus."

Shannon keeps spraying, over and over, and shouts, "I don't care. You quit hurting my daddy!"

The door bursts open (again), and in comes Becky, flanked by two guys who look like mafia hitmen genetically bred with sumo wrestlers.

"Security's here! Who's the—oh, my God, Jamie! Jamie, what happened to your face, sweetie?"

Jamie?

Becky kneels down and the security guys, me, Jason and Dad all crane our necks to get a view of the massive expansive of thigh and purple garters we're invited to enjoy.

Shannon whaps me. Marie gives Jason a little kick and he grunts but doesn't say a word.

"What's *that* for?" he and I ask in unison.

Marie and Shannon give twin snorts while Becky fusses over Dad and helps him to stand.

Jason reaches up toward Marie for assistance in standing. She pretends he doesn't exist, crossing her arms and giving Shannon an unreadable look.

Bad dogs always know when they've been bad and don't whimper. Jason stands on his own and brushes himself off, trying to maintain a thin veil of normalcy, as if he didn't just get into a physical fight with the richest man in Boston, and Dad didn't just insult four generations of Jacobies.

"I assure you," Dad growls, "I am *not* fucking your wife."

"That's right," Shannon says defiantly. "You're much too old for *Jamie* to sleep with, Mom." Her glare at Dad as she repeats the nickname could double as a chemical peel in the finest spa in one of our luxury hotels.

"Shannon, what do you think you're doing?" Dad says to her, whirling on one heel and ignoring Becky's aid. "I'm your boss and—"

Spritz.

Shannon sprays Dad in the face.

I burst into laughter.

"You're a dog. A dog who only sleeps with women who are four or younger in dog years," Shannon announces.

Becky gasps and says, "I'm not four! I'm nineteen."

"I rest my case," Shannon announces.

Dad moves aggressively toward Shannon, who holds up the water sprayer in defense.

"I will not be insulted like this on my own company property!" Dad thunders.

"And you won't yell at my daughter like that!" Jason roars back.

"And I'm not sleeping with Jamie!" Becky adds.

"One of these things is not like the other," Marie sings under her breath.

Marie appears to do math in her head, then turns a shade of angry pink. "Not only are you a cruel parent, but you're an ageist misogynist with little penis syndrome!" she says to Dad, who is trying to decide which of us he's most pissed off at. It's a rare moment when I am *not* in the running, so I'm basking in the glory.

Jason looks like steam is about to come out through his ears, and he yells, "How in the hell do you know that he has a little penis?"

"I do *not* have a little penis!" Dad screams. Marie wins.

Becky turns to me so earnestly, so sweetly, and says, "He's right. He doesn't."

I wish I could try out that fainting trick Shannon just used, but instead I'll just yell like everyone else.

"THAT IS ENOUGH!" I shout. Time to stop observing. Time to take charge with words and actions.

Everyone comes to a halt except for Tweedledee and Tweedledum, who keep chewing their gum and looking bored, like this is the lamest security issue they've ever had to answer.

They're right.

"You," I say, pointing to Marie. "You betrayed my trust."

"I did no such thing!" she protests. "I just went home and thought about what you said at your mother's grave yesterday—"

"You were at Elena's grave?" Dad asks in a small, hushed voice. Somehow, it's worse than when he was screaming.

"Who's Elena?" Becky asks.

"Shut up," Dad and I say in unison.

Becky storms out.

"And you," I say to Jason. "You are making a fool of yourself. Dad and Marie aren't having an affair. Dad doesn't date anyone under thirty and he never dates married women."

"Their expectations are too high," Dad explains.

"I really dodged a bullet with you, didn't I?" Marie says to Dad, then turns to look at Jason with a contrite expression.

"Then why were you joking about marrying Declan's father the other day? And why are you here in James' office, so angry and passionate?" Jason asks, bewildered.

"The joke was mine," I say gruffly. "Poor taste."

"That's easier to believe than the idea that I would sleep with her," Dad says with a sour face.

"You'd be lucky to sleep with me, buddy," Marie shoots back.

"That's right," Jason mutters. "Wait. No," he backpedals.

"Everyone's having sex but me," I say under my breath. Shannon kicks my ankle.

"Hold on, hold on. Go back. Why was Marie talking with you at your mother's grave?" Dad asks. There's a look of genuine concern in his eyes, at least, the part of his eyes that I can see. His right eye took some kind of graze and it's swelling up.

"I went to talk to Mom," I say, keeping it simple.

"You mother is dead," Dad says with great skepticism.

"I never said she talked back."

Silence.

Broken by—who else?—Marie. "Declan told me the story of how Elena died. How Andrew nearly died. And how Declan had to make an impossible choice. Defy his mother's wishes or let his brother die."

Everyone seems stunned. They *are* stunned. She summed it up quite well.

"And how does that relate to my 'cruel parenting,' as you called it?" Dad asks Marie in a cold voice.

"You made Declan feel like he killed his mother," Marie says, chin up, eyes locked on Dad's. "He didn't. He saved his brother. He did what he was told by Elena, who loved her children so much she sacrificed herself for Andrew. That's what a good, loving parent does."

Dad looks like someone slapped him. He actually does—there's a red imprint of Jason's hand on the side of his face, but his expression is also one of shocked reflection.

Andrew slips quietly into the room, the two security guards and Becky behind him and a gaggle of office workers huddling in the hallway, rubbernecking.

"Of course you didn't kill your mother," Dad says quietly, turning to me. "I know that. The wasps did."

Shannon winds her arm through mine, as if she needs to hold me up. She doesn't, but the warmth of her body reinforces me. Like having backup troops appear at the height of battle. You probably don't need them, but just in case...

Dad's bemused look teleports me back eleven years to a very different expression on his face. Back when his eyes were dead and the only feeling he seemed capable of expressing was anger.

I'm eighteen again (this is getting old...) but in the space of a few breaths I realize that's wrong.

I'm a grown man.

"You told me," I say with deliberate elocution, as if saying each syllable perfectly will drive home the emotional truth, "that it was my fault Mom died."

The room becomes an icehouse. Jason's head jolts and he looks first at Dad, then at me. His eyes fill with compassion.

The hardest part is accepting that.

"I never said that," Dad protests.

After closing the door behind him and waving Becky away, Andrew says softly, "Yes, Dad. You did."

Everyone is looking at Dad. I try to catch Andrew's eye but he won't even glance over here. Showing any emotion now, or giving a tell that makes him vulnerable, can't be allowed.

But he can be my ally. Testify. Validate.

"I don't remember ever saying that," Dad says slowly, looking at the floor as if trying to recall a memory. "Perhaps I said something else and Declan misunderstood."

"Declan didn't misunderstand anything, Dad. I remember. I was in the hospital and was recovering and you were making funeral home arrangements for Mom's body."

Dad goes pale. I feel my own face go cold. Moments like this don't happen in our family. We don't reminisce, or process events, or talk about feelings. There's no playbook for how to act. We're all winging it.

Me most of all.

"The doctor came in to review my case and you asked whether I'd really needed the EpiPen. Whether Declan could have just injected Mom and if I'd have been okay with what the EMTs had once they got to us."

"I was trying to understand the facts, Andrew," Dad says in a rough voice. "Trying to make sense of the whole situation."

Andrew acts like he was never interrupted. "And the doctor said maybe. Maybe. That no one can predict how these reactions work, and that while my throat had closed up and I'd lost consciousness, perhaps...maybe...it was possible...nothing could be ruled out...." Andrew uses a sing-songy voice that is so uncharacteristic it seems like mocking.

Dad looks up sharply and stares at Andrew, but his face is anything but comedic.

"And then you lost it when Dec came into the room. You screamed at him so much that hospital security called the chaplain, and she had to take you to her private office."

His eyes are downcast but not in submission. In anger. "You were drugged up, Andrew, full of all the medications they threw into your body to manage the anaphylaxis. I was bouncing between the morgue and your hospital bed. I'm sure you misremember."

"Why do you assume that everyone but you has a faulty memory of that day, James?" Shannon asks.

"Because...I..." James McCormick doesn't get flustered. Andrew and I look away. It's like seeing Dad naked.

Jason, Marie and Shannon are all looking at Dad, and while Jason's look is still one of general annoyance, it's Marie and Shannon who are most interesting to watch right now. They're both calm, heads tilted to the left like they synchronized it, and they're compassionate. Interested. Non-judgmental right now.

Whatever has just unfolded between Dad, Jason, Marie and Shannon over the past few minutes, it appears that Marie and Shannon are ready to listen and process and problem solve this emotional nightmare.

What planet are they from?

Shannon carefully sets down the water sprayer and takes a few steps closer to Dad. She reaches out with a feathery touch and rests her hand lightly on his forearm. His suit is wrinkled and his cuff link has popped off that cuff, leaving the shirt a mess.

"James, I can't imagine the kind of grief you felt that day." Her eyes are warm with feeling, and I can tell there are unspilled tears pooling in them. "No one here is judging you for what you said that day."

Dad looks right at Marie and ignores Shannon, though I can tell from the way he holds his shoulders that she's softening him.

"Marie is," Dad says.

"I don't judge you for what you said that day, James. But I do judge you for spending all these years blaming Declan and making him carry that burden. I've been incredibly imperfect as a parent—"

Shannon and Jason's very loud, shared snort makes Marie jump a little.

Dad buries a smile and so does Andrew. I see it all peripherally but I'm so focused on Shannon. She's like an emotional SWAT team negotiator.

"Anyhow," Marie says primly, "it's the years of blame that you have to let go of if you don't want to lose Declan."

If you haven't already, her eyes say as she looks at Dad.

Andrew and I say nothing but I can feel his eyes shift over to me, a quick glance meant to convey solidarity.

Dad sighs and looks at Shannon's hand, still touching him. "I know what I remember about that day. I remember abject horror. The crush of phone calls from law enforcement and medical authorities no man should ever experience."

Jason's eyes flicker with sympathy and what seems to be a quick, sick recognition that what Dad went through could happen to any man with a spouse and family. Any.

Dad looks at me and I force my eyes to join his. "You were a panicked mess, Declan. I'd never seen you like that. Even as a child you were composed. Calm. Cool. Unflappable. Your mother and I used to marvel at your composure, and wonder if you were hatched and sent to us from some otherworldly place." His face twists into a wistful, morbid grin.

"By the time I found you at the hospital you were wild-eyed and messy, hands covered in dirt and face streaked with tears. You begged me to make them save her. Begged me." He shakes his head. "I barely recognized you. My wife was dead, one son's life hung in the balance and you weren't *you*. Some unseen hand in the universe had dismantled my life as easily as one sweeps a hand across a messy desk and clears it."

I close my eyes but get no relief from the memory. The flash of images behind my eyelids is a movie I never want to see again. Dad's right. I remember the begging. The bargaining. The need to be told that Mom wasn't dead, but even more, the need to be told it wasn't my fault.

"And I snapped," Dad said, looking away. "I'm not proud of it, and while I do doubt that I said exactly what you claim I said, I don't doubt that the emotion behind my words was pretty much the same."

I'm holding my breath without realizing it. So is Andrew. We both exhale at the same time.

Dad's right about one thing: my composure level. A friend in college once told me I'd be the perfect Chief of Staff for a high-level politician because I can stay cool under any situation. And I generally can, because when other people experience stress it doesn't rub off on me. I just watch it unfold and experience it from a distance.

That day when Mom died, though, it was like God himself grabbed a hammer and shattered the snow globe I'd been living in for all my life.

Somehow, I managed to re-instate the composure, but it came at a price. A really big one, involving my dad. He had to be walled off.

Contained. Viewed as a benign threat (I know that's a contradiction, but it works). I'd be friendly. Prove myself to him. Gain his admiration.

But I'd never trust him again.

All eyes are suddenly on me, like I'm expected to say or do something.

No. Dad has to take the first step. Not me.

We wait. And wait. And wait... Shannon gives Dad's arm a light pat and then steps back, embracing me from the side. Her small act of affection conveys so much more to everyone in the room. It's all about solidarity. Validity.

Andrew takes a few steps closer to me, too.

Dad notices it, and he looks at me and opens his mouth to say something at the exact moment someone knocks on his office door.

"Come in," he barks, blowing out a held breath that tells me how tense he really is.

It's Becky. "Mr. McCormick, the FTC officials are here."

Andrew grimaces, and he and Dad share a look. "I forgot today's the day," Andrew says, giving me an apologetic look. "Routine business, but we can't delay."

Marie edges toward me and puts a steady hand on my shoulder, pulling up on tiptoes to kiss my cheek. "Come over for dinner tonight, you two." She turns back to Dad, who is white-knuckling the entire situation from his desk. "You're invited, too." She gives him a smile without teeth and walks over to Jason, her hand linking through his suit-covered elbow.

"You know, I'd like to take you up on that invitation," Dad says while looking down at the papers on his desk, searching for something. He picks up a metal object and fiddles with his wrist, inserting the cuff link expertly. His demeanor has changed. Whatever chance I had at openness or basic emotional recognition is gone.

Thanks, FTC.

"I, for one, would like to start over," Dad adds. He crosses the room and walks right up to Jason, who—to his credit—stands his ground. "I don't believe we've been properly introduced," Dad says, offering a hand. "We'll be sharing grandchildren someday, so the polite thing to do here seems to be a quick handshake and a memory wipe as we pretend none of this ever happened."

I give Dad a nasty look and he instantly realizes his mistake. Marie's eyes light up at his words. Shannon's standing over by the bookcase nervously spraying the same spider plant over and over.

"I hope you'll forgive me," he says to Shannon's parents. I don't think I've ever heard him say those words. It's good to know he *can* say them.

"Deal," Jason says with relief, shaking back. He grabs Marie's forearm and pulls her out of the office.

"Can we expect you for dinner tonight, James?" she calls back. As Shannon and I walk through the doorway, a horrified Becky tracks every movement Marie makes.

"That depends on the FTC, Marie," Dad says, which I know is a firm no. Dad was being polite earlier. There's no way he's coming over to the Jacobys' house, and not just because he's busy.

Dad can't handle real people. One glance at Becky's rack confirms that. Two kickballs suspended under a sheet of Jello shots, covered in a dress.

As I turn to look back, my mind half focused on being a shepherd and making sure the flock is safe and away from the wolf, Dad's eye catches mine. He looks like he has something to say, but then shakes his head with two quick snaps, as if driving the thought out.

Right.

It's probably for the best.

CHAPTER TEN

"I cannot believe I sprayed *the* James McCormick in the face with a spray bottle like a dog," Shannon says, a look of frozen horror on her face. We have said our good-byes to a very embarrassed Marie and Jason and I've brought her into my office to cool down.

"I can," I say. "You took on Dad. One of the richest men in the U.S. Most powerful, too. He could ruin you, and you did the exact right thing. He and Jason were being ridiculous and you—" I gasp, trying not to laugh. Controlling my ab muscles is impossible, though, and Shannon's looking at me with great annoyance tinged with fear.

"He and my dad were just being so stupid! Wrestling on the ground like street punks. They're in their fifties! They should know better! One of them could break a hip!"

"I don't think age automatically means you're more mature, Shannon," I answer. "In fact, I'm damn sure of it."

"I still can't believe I did that."

I smile and hold her, hands sinking into her long, brown hair, which fell out of the clip she wore to work today. "That's my Shannon. You think fast and untangle messy situations." Shannon's completely focused on using the spray bottle on Dad, as if that were the boldest thing she did or said just now. She has no idea that for Dad, it was the least of it. Water evaporates, but emotional truth leaves a mark.

Taking on his perspective of the day mom died was like dropping a nuclear bomb on Dad's internal structure of how the world works. Shannon just told him that if he's the emperor, he's wearing no clothes and might want to check the bottom of his foot for a stray piece of toilet paper.

As her eight-year-old nephew Jeffrey would say, Shannon totally *pwned* Dad.

"This was more than that! This took a kind of courage I don't normally have, to take on your dad like that—" Her hushed tone tells me she's on the verge of tears.

"And that's why I—" *want to marry you*. The words are on the tip of my tongue and I catch them before I blurt them out. A woman who can boldly take on her own father and *my* father like that will be the perfect life companion for the next six or seven decades.

She pulls back and looks up at me with an expectant look. "What? Why you....what?"

"Love you, Shannon." And soon, she'll know just how much.

Her eyes soften and she reaches up to touch my lips. "I love you, too." She shakes her head slowly. "I am *so* fired."

I frown. "No. The opposite. Men like Dad respond to people who stand up to him when he's wrong. After he's cooled down he'll realize you did him a favor."

"A favor?"

"He'll never admit it, of course. And he might give you a hard time here and there for the next week. If you have a meeting with him he'll be extra tough on you. Gruff. Might try to humiliate you, but only once." I think it through for a second. "The audience was fairly small and the stakes were, too. Dad will never forget that you sprayed him like that, but you do realize that because Becky witnessed it, word's going to spread."

"Noooo."

"You're about to get a nickname."

"Like what?"

"The *Jamie* Whisperer."

Her face breaks into four quadrants. One part is trying to laugh. A second is trying *not* to laugh. A third looks like it wants to scream.

And a fourth is just too amazingly beautiful not to kiss.

So I do.

Her body yields under my touch, the thick fabric of her business suit so coarse, covering the lovely soft lines of her curves. The breathy sounds she makes as we kiss transport me. My mind is too full of other people. They take up too much space in my head.

My hands, however, can never be too full of Shannon.

I lift her in my arms and walk a few feet to my desk, where I set her on the edge, her lovely ass on the glass top, my knee pushing hers apart as I grasp her tight, hand sliding under her suit jacket to find her silk shirt. Within seconds I'm touching her hot skin and I groan.

117

"Dec, we talked about this. We're at work, and I —"

My other hand slips between her legs and slides up her inner thigh.

"No, we can't!" she peeps, but she's putting up a feeble protest as her own fingers brush with intent against my fly.

Yes, we can! I think, but now's not the time for campaign slogans. Especially from people I didn't vote for.

I stop, halting at the top of the thigh-high nylon she's wearing, fingers hooked in and ready to pull.

"No?" She can stop me any time. I hold my breath and wait. Patience is a virtue. It might not be *my* virtue, but I can use it to meet my whim when needed.

Her eyes lock on mine. Her hair is mussed and there's this wild-eyed look about her. If she needs permission from me, I'm already there. One word and I'm in her, finding home. The day has left us both splintered and whirling, and I know that we can get ourselves back to center by centering ourselves.

One thrust, one kiss at a time.

"No, we can't," she says again.

And then: "—with an unlocked door."

I break the sound barrier as I cross the room, lock the door, and return to her. She's pulled herself up on my desk and her legs are spread open, inviting me.

She's not wearing any panties. This is becoming a meme, and one I quite enjoy.

Our mouths are hungry, taking and giving, her hands frantic on my belt and fly. Nimble fingers unclothe me just enough. She went on the pill a few months ago so condoms are like the buggy whip. An artifact of a bygone time.

(Yet the whip has a practical use in the bedroom, too, sometimes...).

I look behind her. My desk is littered with business documents and scribbled notes that used to be important but are now impediments. Obstacles preventing me from sinking into her and burying myself in her warmth, my nose in her hair, my tongue loving her teeth.

With one grand sweep I reach behind her and fling everything off the desk.

"Your laptop!" she cries out as the thin, silver computer bounces onto the carpet and makes a distinct beeping sound, like R2D2 protesting being roughed up.

"Don't care," I say, hands pulling off her suit jacket, roaming over her lush breasts. "I can replace it. What I can't do is wait one second longer for this." And with that, she opens herself to me, and the surge of power that has hummed through me finally unleashes. I'm home, warm and fevered, her mouth, her core all mine.

Mine.

She's so damn exquisite under me, the glass-topped oak desk better than any bed, bathtub, kitchen counter, car, limo, helicopter, lighthouse, alleyway behind a piano bar, drive-in, er...*place*...we've ever made love. The flush in her cheeks, the way her eyes dance under her closed eyelids, the thin vein that stretches just past the corner of her eye, and the way she moans my name are all its own reward.

Getting to make love on top of all that is like being handed the keys to the kingdom.

Her hands pull at my shirt and I feel a button pop. Then another. A third as I thrust into her, the power surge morphing into a glow that makes me love her so hard I think my heart is about to thrust inside her, too. Shannon rips my shirt open as her back arches up, her little fingers digging into my chest as she clenches in every way you can imagine.

And that's all I need.

"Look at that city, Shannon. That city is yours," I murmur in her ear, one hand on her jaw, gently turning her head toward the expanse of glass to our side. "Ours. We'll make our mark in the world together."

We're doing incredible deeds *right now*.

Her eyes stay focused on my face, mouth open, tongue caught against her top teeth. "You're the best view I could ever want," she says. "And the only mark I want to make with you is this." Her lips bruise mine as she kisses me, hard, her hands grabbing my back with a frenzy that makes me feel as craved as any man has a right to expect.

Out of the corner of my eye the tops of buildings sprawl in an endless series of brick and steel, pouring out into the back bay like sand on a beach. Enormous and imposing and yet, in the span of centuries and millennia, just grains of sand.

Eternity makes everything insignificant. Even buildings and empires.

And that is why love is so important.

"You are so perfect," I groan as we crest, my hands and mouth unable to touch her enough, her fingers embedding marks that will remain for three days and leave me with a secret smile every time I see them.

As we climb to heaven and then fall, gently, floating back to earth, the desk becomes an unbearably uncomfortable slab of glass and wood. I pull back to standing, eyes eating up Shannon's disheveled form. We look like something out of a cheesy amateur porno film.

I'm good with that.

Her eyes widen and she looks out the window, then at the door, her bra loose around her breasts, shirt pulled up, skirt bunched around her hips.

"I'm a mess!" she groans, sitting up.

I bend down and kiss her, that succulent mouth like sweet honey poured against my lips.

"You're hot."

"I'm sleeping with my boss at the office!"

"It's a condition of your employment."

She pushes me off her and stands, pulling her skirt down and straightening her shirt. "We just broke about nine Human Resources rules in nine minutes."

"Let's go for ten next time."

"There won't be a next time," she protests, reaching back to hook her bra and readjust her breasts. "It's bad enough everyone thinks I only got a job here because I'm screwing my boss, but to *actually* be screwing my boss at work is just a little too..." She makes a shivering movement that sets the tops of her breasts jiggling.

I start drooling.

Between the fight our fathers just had, Marie's inappropriate dressing down of my dad, Shannon spraying my father and the revelation that Dad is fucking his nineteen-year-old admin, I'd say having a quickie on my desktop is the highlight of the day.

Week.

Month.

Okay...week.

And now she's talking about never doing this again? C'mon. You don't give a guy a taste of the forbidden and expect him to forget it.

She scooches off the desk and looks presentable in seconds. The kiss she plants on my jaw is too chaste. Too perfunctory.

Too little.

As she turns to walk out of the room I grab her. She spins and falls against me, sighing deeply. I know it's not that she has any less desire—she's just freaking out on the inside, overwhelmed by too much input.

Same here, except I deal with these emotions by pounding them out.

Shannon eats ice cream.

I like my coping mechanism better.

"Dec, I seriously have to go."

I kiss her.

"Mmmm, mmmph serious!" she says.

I kiss her again.

She steps on my foot. Ooooo, pain. I like pain.

Now, let me say for a moment here that I know I'm being an ass. And if she demanded I let her go, I would. I just feel like a thousand BBs from a BB gun all shoved inside a large glass jar, being shaken by a hyperactive seven-year-old boy. All that kinetic emotional energy makes me feel the impulse to do something, but I lack the coherent emotional centeredness to know *what* to do.

Doing Shannon is pretty much the only tool in my toolbox.

Well, I have another tool, but—

SPRITZ!

A mist of water smacks my cheek and ear.

"What the hell?" I shout, my palm wet as I reach up and wipe my cheek. Stubble greets me. Damn. It's after five, isn't it? Time for my second shave. My eyes register a spray nozzle and then—

SPRITZ!

"Are you *spraying* me?" I choke out, dodging her before she can get me again.

Shannon's face is determined, her jaw set in self-righteous anger. "You won't stop wrestling with my body, you get the spray bottle."

I'm a little too turned on, suddenly. "I've been a bad, bad dog."

She throws the bottle at my head. I dodge that, too (thank you, Milton Academy fencing instructors...) and laugh.

"You are impossible!" she hisses as she edges toward the door.

BZZZZZ.

I don't want to answer Grace's intercom. I know it's someone in Madagascar ready to scream at me because a website widget is three pixels out of order. Or the New Zealanders complaining the exchange rate isn't favorable and that people don't want to spend $212 for their foreskin-based youth cream but are fine with $199.

"That's why you love me," is all I can say to Shannon as I kick the spray bottle under my desk.

Her back faces me as she storms out, but she pauses in the doorway, manicured hand grabbing the threshold, her other hand on the doorknob. I have so much I want to say right now.

Thank you.
I love you.
You're awesome.
You told my father that I matter.
I have never met a soul as incredible as you.
Your tits are the best I've ever—

Yeah. A lot of emotions inside.

"I do love you," she says under her breath. Turning slowly, she faces me, face flushed, eyes wild. Her body's perfectly composed now, and you'd never guessed that two minutes ago I was between those lovely, creamy thighs.

Her eyes narrow but her mouth widens with a smile that could blind the sun.

And then she's gone, leaving me with a matching grin.

If all goes according to plan, I get *that* woman for the rest of my life.

What the hell did I do to deserve her?

CHAPTER ELEVEN

One day before the proposal...

I'm driving home when the dreaded Text of Doom arrives.

> *Want to come over?*

I text back:

> *No. I refuse to sleep with you in your apartment any more. I'll have the driver come and get you, though.*

I'm in the limo and we're stuck in traffic. Construction in Boston is like a fifth major sport. You have the Patriots, the Bruins, the Celtics, the Red Sox and the Orange Cones.

Shannon texts back:

> *I don't want to come to your apartment. Too boring. And who said I offered to sleep with you? Amy and Amanda and I are playing Rock Band. Come on.*

She really knows how to make it so appealing. Three women with the vocal skills of a paralyzed moose singing songs from the 1980s.

Makes a fundraiser for clean water in the Sudan chaired by Jessica Coffin look like fun.

Plus there's that whole not sleeping with me part.

My phone rings. It's Shannon.

"Why won't you come over?" Her words have a sloppy feeling to them.

"Are you drunk?" I ask, perking up. Hmmm. Hope. "Is this a drunken booty call?"

"No. I mean, yeah, I've been drinking, but no. Not a booty call. We just want you to pick up some Thai food and ice cream. This is a *lazy* call."

Wait a minute. "We" means Shannon, Amy, and —of course—Amanda. Two women who live together and their third arm want me to pick up Thai takeout and ice cream?

I suddenly realize I'm definitely not getting any tonight. This is a Period Errand.

Any man who has been in a relationship with a woman long enough goes through the initiation of The Period Errand. It starts with a sudden craving for ice cream and ends with the Purchase of Shame. You know the one.

Ibuprofen, the super-size box of tampons that is bigger than an NFL linebacker, Reese's cups, and two pints of ice cream. (And neither of those pints is for you).

After you survive the clerk's smirk, you drive home to your woman, who is on the couch wearing her "fat pants" (not my term, don't blame me) and who greets you with eager anticipation and a quick kiss on the cheek.

She then makes love to the ice cream and you're stuck watching some Nicholas Sparks novel adaptation on the Oprah channel while she sobs on your shoulder and begs you never to die.

I've been moved into new territory, I see, as seconds pass and she becomes impatient. I'm now expected to run Period Errands for Shannon's entire female pack.

On some level, that means I've gained some kind of trust from all three women, but on another level I feel like my balls have shriveled to raisins that Ben & Jerry's will put into their new flavor:

Emasculated Marshmallow (Pussy) Whip.

"Please, Declan? Please?" she begs.

I sigh. Heavy is my heart (among other body parts...). I want to see her, and Amanda and Amy are fun to hang out with. The day has been as crappy as I expected, and the idea of drinking a few beers and belting out a Queen or Beatles song sounds about right.

"Fine. Just place the order, and—"

"So, at the store," she adds, the pleading tone long gone. Now that I've acquiesced, she shifts into take-him-for-granted mode. "I need you to get—"

"Ibuprofen and tampons," I say.

"How'd you guess?" she whispers.

"Pure luck."

We get off the phone and I buzz my driver, Lance. He rolls the divider down and looks at me via the rearview mirror.

"Change of plans, Mr. McCormick?"

"Yes. We need to go to Shannon's place. And swing by the Thai place on Route 9."

He smirks. "You need me to go to the grocery store on the way there, too?" Great. The smirk.

127

I smirk back. "Yes, Lance. Only this time, *you* can go in and buy what Shannon and her friends need."

He pales.

I feel better.

* * *

We pull into Shannon's driveway to find a picture of Marie plastered all over Amanda's car. The Viagramobile. Amanda and Josh must have traded cars. Who has the Turdmobile? Carol? Poor Jeffrey and Tyler. It might be funny now, but wait until they hit middle school and their friends start calling them Turdboy.

I make a note to offer karate lessons as a birthday present. That's what uncles do, right?

The thought dissolves as the front door opens.

"You are a God!" Amanda declares as I appear at their doorstep, Lance carrying everything for me. Amanda and Amy descend on him like hungry locusts and he takes in Amy like she's eye candy.

"That's my girlfriend's little sister, Lance. Don't even think about it." I give him a good look. "Besides, she's easily fifteen years younger than you."

He backs off and goes out to the limo. Good man. Then again, Amy's wearing one of those spaghetti-strap tank tops, no bra, and yoga pants that say "bootylicious" across her ass.

Not that I'm looking.

Something protective rises up in me, and I feel a need to grab Jason, a shotgun, and to start cleaning it. With my driver's teeth.

I've never had a little sister before. Suddenly I get a glimpse into the future, my and Shannon's daughter on her first date. I feel really sorry for her first love.

Amy's red curls bounce along with, um, other parts that my driver shouldn't be watching as she takes the food and scampers off to the safety of the couch. I walk in and Shannon greets me with a big kiss. It's sweet and salty, her tongue bold and urgent. A guy could get used to being greeted like this.

"Thank you," she murmurs against my jaw. Her hand reaches up and she scratches my neck. "Long day? You have stubble."

"All men have stubble by ten o'clock."

"Your stubble is thicker than most."

"It's the testosterone. It thickens *everything*." I nudge my thigh against hers so she can feel how thick everything is. She just laughs. Great. I love it when she laughs at my hard on. Just love it.

She's right, though. I generally have to shave a second time before late-day business meetings if I want to look more professional.

"I like it," she says, nuzzling. Mixed signals. She's sending me mixed signals. Why is she coming on to me in a room with Amanda and Amy?

There's only one good reason: she wants something from me. And not sex. This would be so much easier if it were sex. But it's never sex. When a woman you've been with for more than a year spontaneously comes on to you during her period, there's an ulterior motive.

Chuckles approaches me like I am part of the Coast Guard and have a basket to lower from a helicopter to save him from drowning in the ocean. He begins to purr, a loud, rumbly noise that makes Amanda jump from across the room and stare at him. Chuckles never purrs. Only for me.

I pick him up and stroke his fur. We get each other. We're the only men in the room. The testicled have to stick together.

Except he's neutered, so...

"How was your day?" I ask Shannon in a fake voice.

She scowls. "Why do you ask?"

"Because I love you." The only correct response when your testosterone is outweighed by a ratio of 3:1. Chuckles doesn't count.

"This pad Thai is amazing. Thank you, Declan!" Amy calls out from the couch. She and Amanda are digging into a carton with separate forks. They don't even bother with plates. Same with the pints of ice cream. It might say "four servings" on the side but what it should say is "get three different flavors together and four spoons and have at it."

The marketing folks at Ben & Jerry's really ought to do a data blitz and start tracking specific female customers' cycles. Send a coupon out the week before. Think of the uptick in sales.

Hmm. File that one away for future campaigns.

"No problem," I answer Amy, hoping they'll spare the other carton for me and Shannon.

"Hey -- would you grab the extra soy sauce?" Amy asks me. "It's in the cupboard."

I open cabinet doors and stare and a sea of samples. Shannon's idea of culinary delight is anything she can get for free on her mystery shops. A mudslide of soy sauce packets threaten to pour out like a ping-pong ball prank. I grab a handful, shove the pile back in, and close the door.

I'm not marrying her for her cooking.

"Want a beer?" Amanda asks as I plunk the soy sauce on the table in front of her and Amy. She's dressed like Amy, but has a hoodie on. The logo is for a water delivery company I recognize from our facilities division. They deliver thousands of gallons for pool fillings. Her sweatshirt is so oversized it comes down to her knees.

"Sure." She reaches down into a camping cooler filled with ice and hands me a brand that Jason must have left here for his daughters.

"That's clever." I've never seen the cooler in the living room before.

She shrugs. "We're being efficient."

"We're being *lazy*," Shannon and Amy intone together. Amanda's face looks weird. Puffy. Like she's been crying.

The room feels a little too small suddenly. The sound of Shannon popping the top off my beer slows down, as if I'm in the Matrix movies. Every second stretches into ten more and a dawning horror hits me.

This isn't a Period Errand.

This is an Asshole Boyfriend Summit.

Worse—it might be both, combined.

I choke a little as I chug the first half of my beer down in one great gulp. The last Asshole Boyfriend Summit I was forced to attend was back in college, at Harvard. I was not the Asshole Boyfriend (note: the actual man is never, ever in attendance for these summits, and thank God).

The purpose of an Asshole Boyfriend Summit is to gather together as many friends, preferably female, to rip apart the ex to the point where the woman comes to see that she really is better off without him.

It's like being stoned to death in absentia.

I wonder who the asshole is.

"It'll be fine," Amy murmurs to Amanda.

"I can't believe I'm still thinking about him." Amanda's giving me wary looks. I retool my mission. Gone is the goal of a few beers, some Rock Band, and reluctant sex in Shannon's bedroom with three pieces of furniture shoved against her door to prevent a Marie invasion, no matter how unintentional. I say I won't ever have sex with her again in her apartment, but I say lots of things that aren't true.

Turning down a shot at sex? I never put principles above my sex drive. That's for monks and Duggar children.

That said, I'm not about to be the only man in a bowl of estrogen soup when one of them is processing a break-up. That's like being a socialist at a Tea Party rally. Sure, you can be there, but when the crowd gets blood lust in them, who do you think will be scraping tar off their pecs and plucking feathers out of their ass?

Hmmm. Kinky.

Anyhow...I finish my beer and put the empty in the recycling bin in the apartment's kitchen, which is about the size of my mailbox.

Amy and Amanda are whispering and every so often shooting me inscrutable looks. Shannon beckons me to snuggle on the couch and share the spare carton of noodles. I get three bites in before I hear it.

Andrew.

Amy says his name and I realize with a gigantic thud that my brother is the object of this summit.

Holy shit.

A tingling at the base of my skull begins. Pure evolutionary biology. As I share DNA with said asshole, I am now prey among the hunters. Soon I will be asked questions about my brother's romantic activities. I would rather gnaw off my right testicle than—

Okay. Retract that.

I wouldn't.

But talking about Andrew and...seriously? Amanda? in a romantic sense is about as interesting as discussing my dad's latest piece of—

"Quick hogging all the shrimp!" Shannon complains.

I frown. "I've eaten exactly two pieces."

She huffs. "Still..."

I hand her the carton.

Tears form in her eyes.

Oh, man. A Period Errand and an Asshole Boyfriend Summit and my brother? What kind of messed up karma did I earn in a prior life to deserve this?

I wrap my arms around her and whisper, "Should I go? Amanda seems upset."

"She's just..." Shannon shudders with a half-sob, a sigh of relief poking through. "It's, um..."

I put her out of her secret-keeping misery. As Winston Churchill says, when you're going through hell, keep going.

"This is about Andrew."

She jerks in my arms. "Has he said anything about her?"

"What? No." The only thing worse than talking about my brother's sex life is being pumped as a conduit for information about his sex life. I need a shower. In a vat of napalm.

She shoots her eyebrows up and wipes her eyes. All business now, she interrogates me like I'm a perp in an episode of Law & Order.

"You're sure he's never talked about her?"

"I am."

She glares. Ten seconds pass. Twenty. Fifty. Countless more. I can win staring contests. I can.

My eyes shift to her boobs.

There. The staring contest is so much easier now.

She waits me out and crosses her arms over her boobs. Boo. I hold fast, though, and it's Shannon who speaks first.

"They should definitely hook up," she says.

"Yeah, Andrew's always been a boob man."

Silence. Oh, shit.

"You stare at *Amanda's* breasts, too? It's bad enough Andrew does, but—" Shannon interrupts herself, her face contorted into a mask of agony. She's looking at me like I decapitated a baby panda on live television and had Gordon Ramsey turn it into sashimi.

A muffled scream from one of the other women in the bedroom tells me I've crossed a line, but my flailing Man Mind can't figure out quite what that line was. Amanda will be part of the wedding party assuming I didn't just destroy the proposal and our entire future together by commenting on Shannon's best friend's breasts. I need to fix this. Now.

In business meetings I am the calm one under pressure. Surrounded by a horde of hormonal women I am nothing but a pile of masculine fail.

Which means I have to pretend to be all dominant and confident. It's my only hope. Cocky and arrogant work when you need them most, as long as you're okay with looking like an asshole.

I'm comfortable with that.

Selective lying helps, too.

"I stare at everyone's breasts," I announce in a loud voice. "I'm a man. We're programmed to do so. It's an evolutionary trait."

"Because of breastfeeding?"

"Because....breasts." I look at her like she's crazy, because she is. I mean...breasts. That's all you need to know, right? Breasts are the female body equivalent of those little curved muscles at the hip on cut men's bodies (and I have those, you know). You can't explain why they're hypnotic because....

Breasts.

No cry of outrage accompanies my statement, so I think I'm safe. I grab Shannon's arm and pull her gently, but firmly, to the front door.

"Look, I don't want Amanda to hear any of what I said, not because it's wrong to say it, but because I don't need a group of hysterical women about to

135

pump themselves up on a rewatching of *Return to Me*—"

She gasps. "How did you know that's the movie we're planning to watch?"

So much for Rock Band. I knew this was a trap.

"—to berate me for saying the obvious. Andrew likes Amanda's rack," I finish.

"He is also driving her nuts with mixed signals," Shannon hisses furiously.

"They're grownups. Let them work it out between the two of them."

She looks at me with utter confusion, like I'm...

Breasts.

"What are you talking about?" she asks.

"Stay out of it," I suggest, my voice slow with intent. "Whatever attraction they have for each other will work its way out."

"I don't understand."

"Don't get involved."

She throws her hands up in the air. "It's like you're speaking another language. What do you mean?"

A cold gong rings through my body.

Shannon is half Marie, right? This is the Marie part coming out.

I grab her shoulders and try a different tack, locking my eyes on hers. "What, exactly, did Andrew do?"

"Nothing."

"Huh?"

"He did nothing."

"He's in trouble for doing nothing?"

"Exactly."

My tiny little raisin balls ache with confusion. "I do not understand."

She makes a derisive sound in the back of her throat. "Men."

"'Men'? What the hell does my being a man have to do with the fact that you're skewering my brother for doing nothing with Amanda?"

"That's the whole point!"

"Who's on first?" I joke.

Her jaw drops as if I've slapped her. Shannon's lower lip quivers and she looks away, her head bowed down.

"I think you should go, Declan. Now's not a good time."

That gong chimes louder inside me.

"I—" I really don't know what to say. No, seriously. This entire hour is like something out of a Tommy Wiseau movie.

The only thing that would make this any weirder is if her mother appeared and—

"Hello!" calls out a familiar voice, the front door behind me opening.

In walks Marie.

"You on your period, too?" Shannon snaps at her mom.

"My period? No. Honey, that ship sailed a long time ago. Your poor father rode the red tide for three decades, and he can retire the crimson pirate mustache now." Marie stands on tip toe and gives me a kiss on the cheek after leaving that statement hanging in the air like a silent-but-deadly bit of flatulence.

She really knows how to make an entrance.

The tension between me and Shannon must be palpable, because as she reaches to give Shannon a hug, Marie says to no one in particular, "Lover's spat?" She finishes embracing Shannon and turns to look at me, her arm around her daughter.

"We're fine, Mom," Shannon says through clenched teeth.

Marie cranes her neck around Shannon and looks back where Amy and Amanda are whispering. She sniffs the air. "Ooo, Thai!"

"And ice cream," I add. Shannon just looks at me, the neutrality in her stare unnerving.

"Marry a man who brings you period food and who....oh." Marie's voice drops off and she leans closer to me, waving Shannon in. We huddle.

"Are you two fighting because Declan doesn't like to—"

"No," I snap.

"I just meant were you—"

"No."

"Are you sure? Because I understand that some men are squeamish—"

"No."

"Do you mean no, you don't, or no, you—"

"No. I'm not going to talk about this with you, Marie. No, I draw a boundary around certain topics with you. No, I refuse to let you bulldoze over my privacy, no matter how good your intentions." The whispering in the other room has stopped.

My voice rises as I add, "And no, I'm not going to talk about my unwillingness to talk about it."

I engage Resting Asshole Face.

Marie blanches.

Then she blinks slowly, turning to Shannon with a pale face but resigned eyes.

"Any Pad Thai left?"

"Declan's half," Shannon says, pointing to the abandoned carton on the table.

Ouch. Now I feel like a jerk. How can I go from being the Period Errand Savior to a jerk in an hour?

Because I'm in a relationship. That's how.

I lean over and give Shannon a kiss on the cheek. "I love you. I'll...we'll talk later."

"Yes. We will." She sighs. "Love you, too."

"Oooooooo!" Marie squeals as she holds the carton of noodles in one hand and a DVD case in another. "*Return to Me*. One of my favorites!"

That's my cue to leave.

CHAPTER TWELVE

A few phones calls on the way home and by the time I get there, Andrew's made himself comfortable on my couch, feet up on the leather, a beer sweating in his hand.

"Make yourself at home," I grumble.

"Always," he says with a smirk. His hand fishes around a bowl of chocolate-covered pretzels and...cheese curls.

Combined.

"You on your period, too?" I ask.

"What?" he calls out, distracted by the baseball game on my television.

"Never mind." Beer sounds good. Great. Give me ten of them and a memory wipe and maybe I can salvage the night.

The first cold swig turns into gulping half the bottle and I plop down next to him. "So what the hell's going on with you and Amanda?"

Have you ever seen a spit take in the movies? Yeah, me too. In the movies.

I've never been the recipient of a spit take.

Until now.

Andrew sprays my legs with beer.

"What?" he chokes.

I grab a fistful of his snack monstrosity and dump it in my mouth. A few chews later and I have to grudgingly confess it's damn good. If I were a woman with monthly cycles I'd chow this stuff down.

Andrew has no hormonal excuse.

"The estrogen crew were having an Asshole Boyfriend Summit and you were the guest of honor. In absentia."

If he had another mouthful of beer it would shoot across the room and spoil my screen. "What are you talking about?"

I shrug. "No idea. But Shannon and I are fighting now and your DNA is infecting me."

"Speak English." He finishes his beer and snatches the snack bowl away from me.

"I am an asshole by association. You're a McCormick, I'm a McCormick, and you pissed them all off."

"I'm not—I just—I...hell. What did they *say* I did?"

"Nothing."

"Well, that explains everything doesn't it?"

"What kind of 'nothing' did you do?"

He shifts on the sofa, suddenly uncomfortable. Uh oh. This is deeper than I expected. If Andrew were *shtupping* Amanda he'd make a joke, or brag about it. The quiet discomfort is unsettling.

He's going to talk about his feelings.

I'd rather talk about riding the red tide with Marie.

"I never called. That's all."

"Since when?"

His face tightens. "June."

"Two months?" Ouch. Poor Amanda, but...

142

"Wrong June."

"*Fourteen* months? You slept with my girlfriend's best friend and didn't call for fourteen months? You sick bastard. I'm ready to go back to Shannon's with a tray of crab rangoon and three dozen chocolate-dipped Oreos to beg forgiveness for my genetic waste of a brother on behalf of all men."

"I didn't sleep with her."

Oh. Huh.

"Why not?"

He swallows, his Adam's apple bobbing. Andrew looks like a nervous teen.

"It's...um..."

Aw, shit.

"You're in *love* with her?"

"No!" The word is fierce and desperate. Aha.

"You're in love with her tits?" I shove the beer bottle in my mouth before he can scream at me. The long line of beer, like an unfurling ribbon, feels so good.

"I, no, well...yes. I mean, you know."

We nod and say in unison:

"Breasts."

"Right," he adds. "We just had this moment and then it felt like it might turn into a thing and I don't want a thing."

"You don't want a thing? You have things all the time."

"Things without strings, sure. But not things with —"

"Women who expect actual reciprocity and mutual respect."

"Exactly."

For the second time tonight, I'm left wondering if I'm in a Tommy Wiseau movie.

"So you dumped her—"

"There was nothing to dump! We shared a kiss."

"A kiss." I snag a chocolate-covered pretzel from the bowl and ignore him as we watch the Sox score a run.

"Just a kiss," he says absentmindedly as we watch the slow mo repeat. "And it's all your fault."

"*My* fault?"

"Your fault."

"I forced you to shove your tongue down Amanda's throat?"

He ponders that for a second, then shoves a handful of food in his mouth. "Yep," he mumbles.

He looks so much like Dad right now I'm creeped out.

"How, exactly, did I manage that feat of physics?"

"By being a douchebag to Shannon."

"When?" I'm man enough to admit that yes, I have been a douchebag to Shannon at various times. Pinpointing exactly which time is an art.

He gives me a hard look. "When you dumped her."

Clear as a bell, because I only dumped her once. And technically, for the record, I didn't dump her. I just, well, we had words. We had words because....

Okay. Fine. I own my stupidity.

"You mean after she pretended to be Amanda's wife and..." I wave my hand. "That."

"Right." He mimics me. "That. When you were a douche."

144

"We've established my douchebaggery. What does *that* have to do with you kissing Amanda?"

"I need another beer," he mutters.

"Is this going to be a long story? Because I'm starving," I add. And I realize I really am, because I shoveled three bites of Pad Thai in me at Shannon's before I was so rudely uninvited because I talked about Amanda's tits.

Andrew looks at me like he's reading my mind. He has a look of anger worse than that time I took his Teenage Mutant Ninja Turtle underwear and used them as a hat for the dog.

"Grab me two beers," he says.

"How about a beer and a tequila chaser?" I offer. A perfectly acceptable dinner substitute. If I get him drunk he'll spill his guts. Never underestimate the power of liquoring up your future CEO little brother and getting him to tell you all his secrets. It's like hacking Sony, but you don't have to deal with North Korea to get the dirt.

"Even better."

Two beers and two shots later, I'm Andrew's best friend. In fact, I may be his *two* best friends. He needs a little depth-perception assistance as I slide him a third shot.

"Her lips taste like vanilla and victory," he groans.

We've slipped into 'bad poet' territory here. I surreptitiously take back the third shot.

"Like sugar and spice," he adds.

"Like snails and puppy dog tails," I mutter.

"No." He frowns. "They really don't."

"Why didn't you call her?"

"Why did you ditch Shannon?" He gives me an unfocused eye. "Then again, I wouldn't date a woman who drove a car with a giant piece of shit on it, either."

"She doesn't drive that anymore," I say, tensing. Andrew made fun of that promotional car every chance he got. "Besides, your woman has a bad case of crabs on her—"

"She's not my woman," Andrew argues, fierce and clear suddenly.

I hold up my palms and give him some respect. "Sure. Fine."

He stands up from the tall stool at the long counter that separates my kitchen from the open-concept living room. The counter is one enormous piece of sliced tree, varnished and polished to a high shine, with evenly-spaced lamps that hang from the ceiling, elongated, hand-blown glass from an artisan out in Shelburne Falls near the Berkshires.

I had nothing to do with any of these choices. That's what interior designers are for. But as Andrew stands he bangs his head on one of the glass lamp shades and it goes swinging like Jeffrey at a Little League game, up at bat and whiffing out with majestic grandeur.

I catch the globe as Andrew shakes it out of its coupling, saving it from hitting the mature wood and shattering into thousands of tiny slivers that would bedevil me for months and consign me to no bare feet.

"Nice reflexes."

"That's what *she* said."

Without a word, Andrew staggers to the couch and stretches out. He groans, then says, "That is the most overdone joke. If another guy says that in a business meeting I'm going to *zzzzzzzzzzzzzzzzzzz.*"

And he's out.

If I were the warm, loving, caring kind of brother who nurtured Andrew and really wanted what was best for him, I'd rouse him and make him sleep in the guest bedroom. His neck is bent at an angle and he's going to wake up dehydrated, with a pounding head and a nasty spasm.

Or two. I'm pretty sure that torch he's carrying for Amanda is damn heavy.

Instead, I grab a fleece blanket from the closet and toss it over him, turning out the lights. The hanging lamp still rocks back and forth, millimeter by millimeter, the only movement in my apartment.

I finish my beer, the soundtrack of my life right now the heavy breath of Andrew in slumber. If I want to listen to someone almost snore, I'd prefer they be naked, spooned against me, generous ass a half-promise for more nookie in the morning, and protesting that she doesn't snore as we go for round four as dawn breaks.

Instead, I get my drunk power-broker little brother blathering on about my girlfriend's best friend and a single kiss from fourteen months ago. How is it that one woman can turn us into idiots when hundreds...er, tens...can flow through our lives without attachment?

I take stock of the night.

First, the Period Errand. Then the Asshole Boyfriend Summit.

And, finally, the Bromigod. As oh, my God, what is going on with my brother? Because what the hell was *that*? My night started with a group of weepy lovesick women and ended with a weepy lovesick man.

Can this day be over?

Fuck it. I *declare* it over, walking into my empty bedroom, stripping down naked and crawling between cold sheets that don't make any sense.

Luckily, sleep doesn't have to.

Chapter Thirteen

Something feels off. I sit up, moonlight streaming through the expanse of glass behind my headboard, the ticking silence of the middle of the night grey and ethereal. My mouth is dry and my skin tingles with danger.

My own home isn't safe.

Clicking sounds in the distance pierce my closed bedroom door. I quietly open my closet and pull out the aluminum baseball bat I store in there for moments like this.

Whatever *this* is.

Later, I realize I should have called 911. But when you're in the haze of being woken by a home invasion, you don't think clearly.

Besides, evolution has primed me for this very moment. Testosterone oozes out of my pores. This is a moment men imagine from the time they're small little beasts with superhero capes and nerf guns.

Defending our turf.

Quiet as a ninja, I walk on the balls of my feet, opening my bedroom door and proceeding down the hall. Andrew is silent, too, his feet hanging off the end of my couch, the blanket pooled on the floor beneath him. His mouth is open and he's drooling a little, my nice leather sleek and shiny in the moonlight.

He's useless against the seven-foot, muscled cat burglar who is obviously here to steal my soul and my valuable electronics.

My eyes dart to the door, where an inch of light from the hallway peeks in, illuminating the library table where I dump my mail.

A knee appears, with a shiny high heel at the foot.

Interesting cat burglar.

Then more knee. A thigh. Hips that make hot blood pound through me, the rest of Shannon entering the room on tip toes. She rotates and closes the door with such precision I start to wonder if she breaks into people's houses for a living.

I flatten myself against the wall where she can't see me, and slowly set the baseball bat on a small wool area carpet. We're both creeping around my apartment in silence, but for very different reasons now.

She cuts behind the couch and stands in front of the breakfast bar, slipping off her trench coat.

Oh, sweet merciful universe.

She is naked except for the high heels.

Merry Christmas in August.

Those come-fuck-me pumps are candy apple red and scream out my name. No, really. I can hear them, tiny little voices that only my now-rising-to-the-occasion little head can hear. It's like those shoes communicate on a radio frequency that my testicles can tune into.

And...I'm at attention.

What is she doing here?

"Shannon?" I whisper, stepping out into the moonlight, hoping I don't scare her.

She startles and freezes, hand on one breast over her heart. Her hair is loose and flowing, and she's curled it. She painted her face, eyes big and bright, lips red and stunning.

She shifts her weight to one hip, eager and a little shy, but also bold.

"Let's make up," she says, squaring her shoulders. "And happy birthday!"

Happy Birthday?

Oh, man. That's right. I'd completely forgotten.

Andrew's head pops up from the other side of the couch and he gapes at Shannon. "Dec? You hired a stripper? I knew you and Shannon were on the outs, but damn, man, you can't just—"

"AAAAIIIIEEEEEEEEE!" Shannon screams. If this whole marrying a billionaire and working in corporate America thing doesn't work for her, she has a future in horror films.

"Are you naked?" Andrew asks me, hair standing on end like a Yorkshire terrier got into a fight with a glue gun. "Dude, put your junk away. I don't need to see that," he adds with disgust.

I stand my ground, planting my hands on my hips and making sure my junk is right there.

"My house. My junk. Don't like it? Too bad."

"AAAAIIIIIIIIIIIIEEEEEEEEEEE," Shannon continues, diving behind the kitchen counter and managing to grab her trench coat at the same time. Her little red heels skitter on the marble tile like cockroaches fleeing the light.

I know I should pay attention to her but if I look at her my junk will respond. And if my junk responds, Andrew will have yet more fodder for making fun of me, and given a choice between responding to Shannon's naked form and giving Andrew rope to hang me with, I—

Wait a minute.

What the hell am I doing?

"Now I know why Dad picked me to be CEO," Andrew says with a snicker as he rubs his eyes and stares at my—

"Hey!" Shannon shouts, stopping her screaming. "James isn't that shallow."

Andrew and I just snort.

"Well, okay," she backpedals. "But quit with the *penith* wars."

"Besides," Andrew says, standing and reaching for his belt buckle. His voice is a bit slurred. "Shannon can't really judge who's got the bigger one until she sees—"

"DUCK!" I shout at Shannon, who maddeningly just stands there, snorting, eyes on Andrew.

"Let the better man win," Andrew continues.

"Keep your pants on, bro," I say in a deadly voice. If he goes there, he'll leave me no choice. "And you," I say to Shannon. "Didn't you hear me? Duck!"

"Quack quack," she says, eyes on Andrew's hands as he unbuckles and unbuttons.

"Shannon!"

She shrugs. In that moment, she looks exactly like her mother.

She gives me no choice. He doesn't, either, because now I see his Calvin Klein-like form as he pulls his pants down and—

I tackle my own brother.

"Your junk is touching me!" he squeals. We're wrestling on the ground now, the button of his jeans scraping against my arm. I grab at his belt buckle to pull his pants up.

"That's what *she* said," Shannon mumbles.

Andrew stops cold.

"No. Just....no. Can we put that joke to bed?"

"We need to put *you* to bed," I growl.

"That's not some kinky offer for a threesome, is it? Because, dude, I'm not into that—"

I jump off him and go into the kitchen for a beer or a cyanide tablet. Whichever I find first.

"Of all the times not to have a spray bottle," she says. "You two are being ridiculous."

"Andrew's being *drunk*," I declare, pouring myself a double shot of pisco and giving it a quick death down my throat.

"I'm not drunk," Andrew shouts as he grabs the television remote and tries to swipe the buttons. "Hey! What happened to my phone? It's broken. I need to get a ride home."

Shannon stands and pulls a phone out of her boobs. It's like watching a magician pull a rabbit out of a hat, because she's naked and wearing only a trenchcoat.

"Which driver is it tonight?" She knows how our limo service works.

"Gerald."

"Calling now. He needs to leave." She holds up a finger as the call goes through and within twenty seconds Gerald's on his way. "And," she adds, "So do I." She reaches into her trenchcoat and grasps her car keys.

No.

NO.

"If we're riding in the same limo," Andrew says as he struggles to button up, "do you mind if we stop at that twenty-four hour Greek place? I'm starving. And my head feels like someone dropped a forklift on it."

He slumps down on the couch and is snoring in seconds.

Shannon looks at him with a pained expression as she clutches her coat closed. Her phone has magically disappeared. Her eyes turn to me, slowly cataloguing the landscape of my body. I don't mind. This is the first chance we've had to talk since Andrew so rudely interrupted us, and as she looks at me, taking in my legs, then hips, then the part that reacts to all this attention (that would be my *heart*, you gutter-minded naughty beast...), I remember that she started this second act of our night with the phrase "Let's make up."

"You came over to—" I almost say "apologize" but realize that would be a catastrophic mistake.

"To try to mend things," she replies in a quiet voice. Distracted. She's really watching me. I have no self-confidence issues, no self-consciousness being naked around her. Around anyone, really. You play enough sports at a prep school and in college and you get used to being nude around other people. It's

154

a kind of armor. Being shy gives people the impression that you have something to hide. Something to be ashamed of. Something to pick on.

I look down at my own body, eyes crawling over the same flesh she's observing.

Nothing to be ashamed of here.

From the look on Shannon's face, she seems to agree.

"I'm sorry," I say with a slow sigh, realizing I'm the one who has to cross the gap. After all, she snuck into my apartment in the dead of night wearing nothing but a coat and high heels.

That's the male equivalent of the best apology *ever*. She doesn't need words.

Her eyes don't meet mine. They're stuck somewhere on my hips, looking at my ass.

I tighten it.

Her eyes widen, pupils dilating.

Hold on.

I thought women weren't aroused sexually from visual cues. Has *Men's Health* been lying to me all these years? *Esquire*, too? All those magazines I've been stuck reading in doctor's offices or international business lounges with crappy Wifi say the same thing: women are slower to warm up. Women aren't aroused by images and videos. Men are programmed to be turned on by what they see, women by what they feel emotionally.

A lovely red flush covers Shannon's face and chest as she finally drags her eyes to meet mine.

I'm about to marry an outlier.

Attagirl.

Then: *Bzzzzz*.

155

Shannon's breasts vibrate. She reaches in and grabs her phone, holding up the screen.

"Gerald's here."

"Please stay," I beg as Gerald knocks on the door.

Panic fills her face. "Shouldn't you put on a robe?" She reaches into her coat and buttons something, then tightens the sash around her waist.

Now she looks like any other business woman on the street in the Financial district. Except for the sexy shoes.

I look down at my body. "Why? Gerald's seen it." To prove a point, I go to the front door and open it. Gerald's standing there, face impassive.

"Evening, Mr. McCormick," he says, looking past me. "Is your brother ready?"

Gerald doesn't even twitch at my nakedness.

Shannon, however, grabs my arm and drags me into my bedroom.

"You can't do that to people!" she hisses, rifling through my bathroom and coming out with a blue robe she gave me for Christmas.

"Do what?"

"Be naked in front of them."

"You don't like it when I'm naked in front of you?"

"Not me. Andrew. Gerald."

"Andrew came over last night, ate period food, got drunk and cried about Amanda half the night, passed out on my couch and suggested a threesome. I can do whatever the hell I want to do in front of Andrew, Shannon."

"But poor Gerald!" Her eyes narrow. "Wait. Period food? Cried about Amanda?"

156

I ignore that part. "Poor Gerald is a sculptor when he's not driving a limo. I've been a model for him before."

"Quit making stuff up!"

"I'm not. I don't lie, Shannon." We're veering into very explosive territory now.

"I didn't say you were lying. It's just...unnerving. How you feel like you own the world."

Ah. *That's* what this is about. A flash of our very first dinner together courses through me, turning from image and memory to blood and bone.

"You're upset with me because I feel like I have the right to have my own opinions and to be confident in them." I don't phrase it as a question.

"Sometimes you don't think about how other people will feel when you—"

"Because I don't."

"You don't care?"

"I don't think about other people when I'm doing or saying something that is true to myself."

Confusion clouds her face. "That's so..."

I reach for her hands, my warmth in stark contrast to her chilly fingers. Maybe I can transfer some certainty along with a little heat. "It's not that I don't care about other people's feelings. It's that I don't think about other people when I'm making a decision about who I am."

"There's a difference?"

Her question hangs in the air between us.

"Mr. McCormick?" Gerald calls out. "I have your brother ready to go. Is Ms. Jacoby coming as well?"

My eyes burn, matched by her intensity as we look at each other.

"Please stay," I ask, turning away and walking out to where Gerald has Andrew drinking a cup of coffee, leaning against the wall in front of the main door.

He grunts a hello and stares at his cup.

"You need help?" I ask Gerald, eying Andrew with skepticism. He's got more muscle on him than you'd think, and when it's deadweight...

"No, he's fine." I hear Shannon's shoes *click clack* on my floor behind me. Gerald eyes me in my robe, then looks at Shannon. He's smarter than he looks, but that's because he looks like a pile of lightly-baked bread dough shoved together to form a human being. You'd never guess a guy that big and burly has the heart of an artist in him.

"I don't need a ride home," Shannon says quietly, her hand pressing into my shoulder, rubbing in circles over the terrycloth robe.

I relax.

Gerald's face changes into what passes for a smile. He looks like bread that's split down the center and baked. "As long as you're fine, then. And Mr. McCormick?"

Andrew and I both answer, "Yes?"

Gerald eyes Andrew up and down. "I meant Declan." He looks at me. "We're starting a new session for nudes next month. If you're not traveling too much, the class would really appreciate having you model again."

"Again?" Shannon says, clearing her throat pointedly.

Andrew's just staring at his cup of coffee like it's the Oracle of Delphi.

"Sure," I answer. "Just call Grace and set it up for me."

"Will do." And with that, Andrew and Gerald are gone and I'm blissfully alone with a woman who is looking at me like she just caught me with lipstick on my collar and a blow up doll with painted lips.

"You're a nude model for art classes?"

"In my spare time." I try disarming her with my most charming smile.

I fail. "*I* am supposed to be your spare time. You barely have time for dinner most weeks, but you can prance around naked in front of a bunch of women and women who use their hands to recreate your ass —" She continues her nagging, but that's all I really needed to hear.

Ah, jealousy.

It cures so many ills.

Women hate jealousy in their men. Oh, they want a touch of it—just enough to feel wanted. Special. Craved.

Men, on the other hand, love it when their women get jealous.

It means we get more sex.

Makes no sense, but there it is. As Shannon's heated rebuke continues I try to hide my self-satisfied (she would call it *smug*) smile, but I fail.

"Don't laugh at me!"

I grab the sash of her coat and yank it open, pulling wide the two sides of the coat with a snap that sends her buttons flying.

"Dec! What are you doing?"

159

Oh, I think it's clear what I'm doing.

I pull her coat off, drop my robe, and pick her up in my arms.

"Hey! Put me down! We're talking! I have more to say—"

I cut her off with a kiss, then throw her on the bed.

"You can't just—"

Another kiss. She moans, that kitten-like little sound so sexy in the back of her throat. She starts to kick her heels off and I break away.

"Leave them on. Consider it my birthday gift."

"But I have a birthday present for you!"

"This is all I need." And it's true. She knows I don't like making a big deal out of birthdays. The fact that she accepts that and doesn't force it is part of why we're such a good fit.

She kisses me this time, then pauses as if she's thought of something.

"What?" I ask, my fingers fully engaged in brilliant make up sex. The rest of my body is about to follow.

"I'm, um....you know. It's the end of that time of the month."

"Never stopped me before."

"You don't mind?"

"Shannon, there is nothing about your body that I mind."

And then I show her how true that is.

* * *

"You could model with me," I inform her in the morning as we wake up with bed head and hot abs. The slopes and valleys of her body deserve to be permanently preserved for antiquity. For future generations to gasp and admire. She's warm and soft and best of all—mine.

She snorts. "I'm about as likely to do that as I am to learn how to ski."

"You don't know how to ski?"

"I like having intact knees and living without a traumatic brain injury. I'm weird that way."

"Marie and Jason never took you?"

She gets quiet, a lazy finger making trails over my chest. "It's expensive. Amy was on the school ski club, but no. Not me. We didn't have the money back then. I tried once, with Steve. I'm still in therapy to get over it," she jokes.

Steve. The Ex. Just who I want to have mentioned while we're naked in bed.

"Besides, I'm a natural klutz."

"You're really not," I stress. "No one who can use a tongue, lips, two hands, a nipple and a toe like you did last night all at the same time can be accused of having poor coordination of any kind *whatsoever*." Her comment about money makes me resolve to have Grace book us for a series of ski weekends in Stowe at a place with good lessons, an oversized hot tub, a giant stone fireplace and room service. Shannon might even make it to the slopes for an hour a day.

She slaps my chest and tweaks my nipple before she's off, ass all I can see, and then she's gone.

"What are you doing?"

161

"Making coffee."

It's like I've been handed someone else's good karma.

I slide my arms behind my head and stare at the ceiling fan, running through the day's events. Tonight is it. Greg's supposed to have set everything up, and we go to Le Portmanteau, but Shannon hasn't said a word. As soon as she heads out for work I'll give him a call.

Carrying two mugs full of steaming coffee, Shannon comes back into the room with a funny look on her face.

"So, about tonight. Are you free?"

This is taking an interesting turn.

I sit up and take the cup she offers me. Propping a bunch of pillows against the headboard, I pat the empty space next to me. She nestles in and we sit like an old married couple, starting the day with a leisurely cup of coffee and an awkwardly uncomfortable conversation about—

"—and Greg needs me to do that mystery shop."

Our future.

"He what?" I ask, pretending to be angry. She brought this up the other day, the same day our dads decided to turn into pro wrestlers, but I feign ignorance.

"I know," she soothes. "I know he promised and I promised I wouldn't do any more mystery shops for him, but this is the one I mentioned earlier. Le Portmanteau."

"I had children pee on me so I could get that promise," I remind her. Last Christmas Shannon stepped in to cover for her sister, Carol, as a mall

10

Santa's elf. Greg had an emergency and roped me into playing Santa for an hour and a half. I'm still having flashbacks after having Shannon's cat, Chuckles, claw my thighs while wearing a reindeer costume and getting into a fistfight with a Russian mobster.

Yeah. It was as weird as it sounds.

Worst of all, I *still* get #HOTSANTA messages on Twitter and a steady stream of pictures sent to me of various people in elf costumes.

Most of which involve candy canes in places you do not want to see.

"I know you did," she says, contrite. "But Greg already set it up."

"Have fun," I say, taking a deliberate sip of my coffee.

"Oh, um...I thought you'd go with me."

"Why would I want to do that? You need help counting the level of paint discoloration on the doorjambs of the coat room?" Mystery shoppers actually do this kind of crap. I only know because Shannon's explained it to me a thousand times.

"I need help eating a delicious meal!"

A meal I'm paying for.

With my life.

I sigh, a sound of frustration that appears to be convincing enough to make her look at me with such earnest persuasion. "Please? It'll be fun. And for once, I'll be the one treating you to an outrageously overpriced meal. Greg says we can get two bottles of wine off the menu and they have to be priced over $100 each!"

Greg is a dead man.

I need to talk to Andrew about having Anterdec just acquire Consolidated Eval-shop so we can stop dealing with all of this mystery shop bullshit. Make him an offer he can't refuse.

"Declan?" Shannon's wide, warm eyes catch mine and I sink into them, her body lush and all mine. She has no idea that tonight is a set up. That I have all the food planned down to the flavored mint toothpicks. That a piece of tiramisu will be delivered with my mom's ring resting at the bottom of a glass of Champagne.

And that by this time tomorrow morning she will be the confirmed future Mrs. Declan McCormick.

I can't keep up the charade.

"Okay. Fine," I say, pretending to concede. "But this is it. No more mystery shops."

"Agreed!"

"And I need another cup of coffee," I mutter. Might as well milk this for all it's worth.

"I was thinking I might find another way to help you wake up," she says as her head disappears underneath the sheet.

So much good karma. *So* much. I must have saved thousands of children or built a hospital in my last life.

I'm coming back as a rat in my next life, aren't I?

Better enjoy this one while it lasts.

Shannon makes sure I do.

CHAPTER FOURTEEN

The Proposal...

Le Portmanteau is designed to make you feel just a little bit like a country bumpkin, even if you're a Parisian sophisticate with a world palate and the budget of a sheik.

That's why it's Jessica Coffin's favorite restaurant, if you believe her Twitter feed.

Not that I read her feed. That's Grace's job. I just get executive briefings now.

Grace made sure Jessica is not here tonight. Having her make a sudden appearance the night I propose to Shannon would not just be catastrophic, it might land my future fiancée in a jail cell for a night.

Which would put a slight damper on our celebration.

Self-preservation has many incarnations.

While I had already cleared my day well in advance, knowing and preparing the perfect proposal, Shannon is running late. I'm standing here in the waiting area tapping my toes like a kid at his first formal dance with a date who's about to stand him up, but he doesn't know it yet.

But Shannon won't no-show.

Right?

Of course not. Women don't wake you up like that in the morning and then leave you hanging twelve hours later.

Besides, four syllables guarantee she's coming:

tiramisu

There is something magical about that dessert. It's like saying the word "breasts" in the company of straight men. "Tiramisu" is a siren call to women.

She'll be here.

I'm on my phone, checking for client email, when the phone rings. Not with a text, but an actual call. That means it's either Grace or Dad, because everyone else texts.

This is a number I don't recognize.

"Hello?"

"Declan McCormick?"

"Yes."

A relieved sigh. "Ah. This is Chandra Mobu, from Le Portmanteau."

I look around, but the only person who works here is speaking with a couple who walked in and are expecting a table without reservations. Amateurs. I—er, Grace—booked four months ago.

"Yes?"

"Giuseppe was the person who arranged your proposal tonight, and he's not here."

A cold rush fills my veins. "Excuse me?"

"I'm very sorry, Mr. McCormick. I'm stepping in to help, and Giuseppe gave me your instructions. He caught the chicken pox from his grandson, and—"

What's up with all these cases of adult chicken pox? First Angelina Jolie, now Giuseppe? Why is chicken pox suddenly ruining some of the most important events in the world?

"Do you have all of my instructions?" I demand, clipped and tight. One problem with relying on other people to help you: they're human. It's an inherent weakness and it's unfailingly annoying. "The toothpicks, the ring, the tiramisu, the Champagne, the—"

"I assure you, we have his directions, and we will make certain this is a proposal you will never forget, and one with great fanfare and excitement."

"Damn right." I shut off the phone and take a deep breath, fists tight, jaw ready to cut glass. The jeweler's box rubs against my thigh, heavy and light as can be.

Like my heart.

Shannon picks that very moment to walk in.

Somehow, she manages to change time itself. All of the air in the room halts its circulation, crowding around her as she looks at me with an apologetic smile. Her hair brushes against her shoulders, hips moving like she's on a runway and I'm the only person in the audience watching her.

Two hands start clapping inside my chest. My throat goes dry. My entire existence revolves around the fact that she is here, right now, and I am about to ask her to share the rest of her life with me. To love me and believe in me and make children with me. To grow old together if we're lucky, and to ache with the pain of loss if we're not.

167

I need her to be the center of my universe because, frankly, I don't have a choice. She's it, whether she says yes tonight or not.

Please say yes.

Because she has no idea what's about to happen, she's remarkably normal, putting her arms around me and stretching up to plant a quick kiss on my lips. "Hi, honey! I'm so sorry I'm late. We had a problem with that new online accounting marketing campaign, and the client was horrendous. As if it's my fault the spokeswoman they chose for the ads turns out to have nude photos of her circulating all over because her psycho Romanian ex-"

She stops talking and looks at me in alarm. "What's wrong?"

"Nothing."

"You're *gray*. And not as in Christian Grey."

"I'm fine."

"Declan, you look like the poster child for how to spot a heart attack." She pulls me back to the chair I was just sitting in.

"I'm fine." My hands feel like ice cubes and there's a lump in my throat the size of China. This is real. This is happening. My confidence is gone. It vanished without a trace. This internal case of the nerves isn't because I'm worried she'll say 'no.'

It's because I realize she's about to say 'yes.' The magnitude of my love for her can't be captured in a number, nor an exponent, nor by any known mathematical equation. It's wider than the galaxy and bigger than any known dimension.

The enormity of who we are and how we're about to join is so vast. I didn't know I could feel this much love for someone.

For her.

"Put your head between your knees."

"I'd rather put my head between *your* knees."

She gives me a surveying look. "All right. You must be fine if you're making sex jokes."

"That wasn't a joke."

She sniffs and sighs. "You've clearly recovered."

"I was never *not* fine."

"Excuse me for worrying you might be having a heart attack."

I kiss her cheek and snuggle up. "Thank you."

"Because that would totally blow my cover for this mystery shop," she hisses.

I feel so loved.

Just then, someone who sounds exactly like Chandra Mobu appears, a petite, dark-haired woman with kind, sharp eyes and a grey streak through long hair pulled back in a pony tail.

"May I help you?" she asks, pointedly not looking at me. I'd warned Giuseppe not to tip Shannon off with any behavior she might detect as abnormal.

My being the color of industrial waste when she walked in doesn't count.

Nearly forgetting the ruse, I start to respond when Shannon elbows me and says, "Yes. We have a reservation."

"What's the name?"

"Jacoby."

Soon she'll just say McCormick. A hot rush of blood pours through me.

My head dips and I can't suppress a smile. Here we go. That's better. This is who I am. Grounded. Calm. Focused.

Utterly sure.

"Mr. and Mrs. Jacoby? Right this way," Chandra says with a gracious smile and a mischievous charm. There goes my jaw again, tight as a drum. *Mr. Jacoby* my ass.

Shannon just snickers and links her arm in mine as we enter the dining room.

Le Portmanteau is as different from The Fort as can be. There's a reason I asked Greg to use this restaurant for this ruse: the last place anyone would ever expect to see me is here. I'm a nobody, because this place isn't our competitor. They're sleek Scandinavian lines, all grey and white with flashes of primary colors, like a Gubi showfloor with an incredible menu, while The Fort is Teddy Roosevelt's Delmonico's steak house for the twenty-first century.

We're seated, and I pull Shannon's chair for her. She's always a little surprised when I do this, even though we've been together for a year and a half. It's engrained in me; Mom made me take classes in comportment and manners. I can dance a waltz, find the shrimp fork, and help an old lady cross the street in ninety seconds or less.

And I speak Russian.

I'm a regular catch.

Shannon's seated and waiting for me to sit, so I do, directly to her left. My mind feels like it's three seconds behind my body.

170

"Wine? Shall I send the sommelier?" Chandra asks me.

With eyebrows raised, Shannon looks at her and says, "I'd love that. Thank you."

Chandra leaves and just as she's out of earshot, Shannon whispers, "Can you believe that?"

"What?"

"The sexism."

My mind turns into slices of Swiss cheese being carved by toddlers with pinking shears.

"The *huh*?"

"The sexism! Asking *you* about the wine. It's so mid-twentieth century." She looks around the half-empty dining area. We're seated right by the huge window that overlooks the ocean, the bay calm and tranquil. As dusk kicks in the waves lap at shore and it all feels very—

"Unbelievable," Shannon chokes out.

I'm starting to agree.

"That's going in my eval."

Let me pause here for a moment and admit that it never occurred to me, in any of my nineteen visions for how my proposal would unfold, that Shannon would actually *do* the mystery shop. I used it as a convenient way to get her here and surprise her.

But for her to be here and take the evaluation seriously is not even in my mental playbook for how this all happens. In my mind we talk, we laugh, we enjoy a bottle or three of wine and a lovely meal, then dessert and Champagne are served with a ring as the coup de grace.

Instead, she's talking about—

"And can you check the men's bathrooms? I'll go if you don't want to deal with it," she adds, reaching for her bread plate and the herbed butter. "But this isn't a bagel shop."

Just then, the sommelier appears. Shannon asks him a few questions about white wines while I silently turn into the Hulk inside my skin.

My rapidly graying skin.

The ring is digging into my thigh so I shift a little, nudging against Shannon's knee. Her eyes dart round the room, take in the gorgeous view, and then rest on me.

"Hi," she says.

"Hi."

"Thank you for coming here tonight. I know it's the last thing on earth you want to do." Her hand comes to rest on my thigh, dangerously close to the ring.

I shift away.

She looks hurt. "I—did I—what's going on?" she asks in a quiet voice.

Saved by the wine steward. The sommelier starts the wine parade with me. Shannon glowers. Wine is poured and soon we have a bigger mess than perceived sexism at a luxury restaurant.

"Why don't you want me to touch you?" she asks as I guzzle my white wine like it's cough syrup and I have TB.

"I do," I protest, pouring myself another glass.

"Then," she croons as her hand goes right back where it was, "why did you flinch?"

I move away. "Because I don't appreciate being objectified and treated like a piece of meat."

"Since when?" she says, a little too loudly and with great incredulity.

"If you can find sexism in a restaurant I can find it in our relationship." I reach under the table and slide the ring so it's squeezed between my legs.

Great. Nothing like feeling like a drag queen with a bad tuck on the night you're about to propose to your girlfriend.

Who is looking at you like you belong on top of her old Turdmobile.

I take her hand and put it back. "There. Happy?" My fake grin isn't helping.

"Declan, what is going on?" she asks suspiciously. "You don't look well, you seem nervous, and you don't want me to be intimate with you." She swallows, hard, then sits up straight and tall. "Is there something you want to tell me?"

"Like what?" Man, this wine is good. I think I'll buy the vineyard. Right now. I'll grab a helicopter and go to Napa. Immediately.

"Are you...unhappy?"

Just then, the server appears, full of hope and promise and a melodic recitation of the chef's specials. I swear it's a performance worth of a poetry slam, in verse. Is that iambic pentameter I hear? A bit of Olde English thrown in for good measure?

Shannon listens politely and orders a salad and fish.

Oh, shit.

I order a thick porterhouse and as the server leaves, ready myself to grovel.

"Can we start over?" I ask just as Shannon stands. "Where are you going?" I ask. Have I blown it so badly she's leaving? And how did I mess this up? One small issue and another small issue and suddenly she's hurt and pissed. It's like—

Like when I dumped her.

Oh, man.

"Shannon, please come back. Let me explain. I'm just really overwhelmed and once you know everything you'll understand."

I'm not doing myself any favors with my word choices. That sounded like my dad trying to explain why Mistress #1 got Mistress #2's roses and note.

She glares. "I need to go check the bathrooms." Before she leaves she grabs her wine glass and guzzles it like a hockey player mainlining electrolytes between plays.

I watch her receding form as it turns down a white hallway, disappearing like my hope for a perfect proposal.

Chandra walks past me and quietly says, "I hope everything is going as planned, Mr. McCormick."

"Not quite," I reply through gritted teeth. I hand her the ring as discreetly as possible. I have to give her credit; she palms it like a pickpocket from "Oliver Twist", so smooth it's as if we never touched.

"Our staff is on it. After your meal we will have the tiramisu and Champagne ready. The string quartet should arrive any minute and will come out as scheduled."

Cheesy, right? I know. But that's how this works.

"Thank you," I say as she nods and disappears, gliding away.

Shannon's on her way back, a too-calm look on her face.

"What was that about?" she asks me as I stand and hold her chair for her, pushing her in.

"Nothing. Just checking to see if everything is fine," I explain.

"Fine," she says. There's a bite to her words. I put my hand on her knee and while she stiffens, she doesn't move.

"Shannon, can we hit the rewind button? I wasn't myself when we arrived, and I'm really looking forward to this evening."

"Since when do you look forward to a mystery shop?"

Oops.

"Since it means having hours alone with you."

Her face softens, eyes turning dreamy. "Really?"

"Always."

Bzzz.

My chest vibrates, the effect like a defibrillator, making me jump. I pull out my phone.

Grace.

I stand and hold one finger up to Shannon, who gives me a withering look, the sweet, loving smile fading fast.

"This is not a good time," I grunt into the phone.

"I know, Declan, and I am so, so sorry, but some guy named Giuseppe keeps calling. Says he needs to talk to you."

Chandra walks by and gives me a surreptitious thumbs' up. "Oh, him. It's fine, Grace. I don't need to talk to him. Everything's under control."

"You sure? Because he's calling from the restaurant where you're proposing and he's insisting it's important."

What could a guy stuck at home with chicken pox need to tell me? "It's all good. No worries."

"Okay. I'll pass on the message. And Declan?"

"Yes?"

"You picked a great one."

"Thanks."

"And happy birthday. How cute that you picked the same day. Smart move. This will make it hard to forget this day."

I try to process a reply, but Grace is off the phone before I can. I'd completely forgotten about my birthday in the planning for this proposal.

Our salads were delivered in those handful of seconds I was on the phone, and Shannon is daintily taking bites that make her look disturbingly like Jessica Coffin.

"You need to leave?" she asks in a resigned tone.

"No." I sit back down and stuff lettuce in my mouth. It might as well be embalming fluid.

She gives me a weak smile. "Good." As she pulls her phone out of her purse, Chandra comes over to the table, making Shannon freeze. I know she's going for her app, hoping to answer some questions from this pseudo mystery shop.

"I hope the food is pleasant?" Chandra asks.

"Great Romaine," I mutter. "The best. Ever."

Shannon's glare could perform Lasik surgery on me from two hundred feet.

Chandra nods and walks over to another table, working the room.

"I do not like that woman," Shannon says, stabbing a tomato viciously like it's Chandra's eyeball.

Entrees appear, freshly-ground pepper is offered, and soon we're in peace, Shannon tapping away on a screen as her fish becomes a smelly piece of rubber. My steak tastes like I'm nibbling on someone's calf, and my stomach is doing the two-step.

And then it hits me.

I can call this off.

Not the marriage itself, but this ill-fated proposal. In business meetings I'm never afraid to hit the pause button or withdraw a proposal altogether to go back to the drawing board and regroup. Maybe —just maybe—that's the best approach here.

Whatever choice I make needs to happen fast if I'm stopping all this, because the gears are in motion. Musicians, tiramisu, ring, Champagne...

Little breathy sounds are coming out of Shannon. She takes two bites of her fish and sighs. Not being a mind reader, all I can do is reach for her hand and take it in both of mine, caressing the soft skin, hoping she'll let me make all of this right.

"I'm sorry," she finally says.

Wasn't expecting *that*. But never look an unsolicited gift apology in the mouth.

"Okay," I say, not sure where this is going.

"I'm just so stressed with work, and I know you hate doing mystery shops with me, and—"

The waiter arrives with the tiramisu and a bottle of Champagne.

Chandra's nowhere to be seen.

Guess calling it off isn't an option now, is it?

Shannon's eyes light up, then die, like a Blue tip match being struck and snuffed out. "What's all this? I didn't order dessert yet."

"Compliments of the house," the server explains.

She gives me a look that says *Have I been busted?* Part of her pride with mystery shopping is that she's undetectable to staff. Being skillful with her evaluations is critical. She looks crestfallen as the piece of tiramisu bigger than my brother's ego is plated in front of her.

Just what every man wants when he's proposing —for his beloved to look like her childhood pet got hit by a car.

Two Champagne flutes come out from behind a server and a cork pops.

Hold on.

SCREECH. Slam on the brakes.

The ring is supposed to be *in* the Champagne before they serve it.

The *glug glug glug* of alcohol pouring from the bottle into the glasses echoes in my mind as I search visually for my mother's ring. It's not exactly a small bauble, so it should be here.

It should be here.

"Enjoy your dessert," the server says, giving me a wink when Shannon's head is tipped down.

Where is the ring?

Where is the fucking ring?

"Do you think they've guessed?" she says in a panicked voice, picking up her fork.

"Guessed what?"

She throws her non-fork hand in the air in frustration. "That I'm evaluating them? No restaurant has ever just spontaneously offered me Champagne and tiramisu!" She pauses to think. "Maybe they recognized you?"

JULIA KENT

The truth is right there. My mouth is full of it. The authentic, verifiable fact that this is all a set up for her benefit—for our benefit—is crouching on my tongue, ready to be unfurled and explained, described and confessed. It coils, waiting for a signal from my brain, hesitating until I decide it's time to say what I need to say.

In hindsight, ten seconds could have made the difference between a delightfully tender proposal and one that ends in blood, pain and humiliation.

I'm a decisive guy.

But not this time.

She carves out a large bite from one corner of her piece of tiramisu, the custard and ladyfinger concoction asymmetrical on the fork, a little too suspicious. Because it's dusk, the only light in the room is candlelight and overhead, dim bulbs designed to give an aesthetic that shouts romance.

Her lips encase the sweet treat and she lifts her full glass of water, taking a big swallow just as her eyes bug out of her head.

I think I just found the ring.

Shannon leaps to her feet, the fork clattering to the ground, her water glass falling as she drops it and clutches her throat.

"Unng! Unng!" is all she can say. A cold wave of horror takes over my body, as if I've been flung into the ocean off a cliff and tossed by a thirty-foot wave.

Chandra appears suddenly and shouts in a commanding voice, "Someone call 911! We need a doctor! Heimlich!"

Two busboys pound through the kitchen's doors but before they can get to us, my arms are around

Shannon. I'm behind her, pelvis against her ass, hands forming the carefully folded fist under her sternum.

She's barely breathing. Her grunts become more frantic, her fingernails clawing at her throat. I can't see her eyes and frankly, I don't want to right now. If I see the glow of who she is begin to fade as this unfolds badly, I can't do what I'm about to do.

In a split second I become two Declans. It's the third time in my life I've had this happen. My second with Shannon. The day she was stung I divided into two distinct realities, each able to watch the other, like viewing a film.

One Declan lifts her into me, ready to thrust up and dislodge the ring. She makes an unholy sound and tenses.

No air.

C'mon c'mon c'mon.

I envision the ring in her throat, willing it to loosen and shoot out of her mouth. Jesus Christ *come on come on come* ON, and just as I'm about to perform the Heimlich, she stops me.

A thin hiss of air comes out of her but she's desperate, leaning over the table, hands on the edge as a man my father's age rushes over, followed by a petite woman with greying hair.

"I'm a doctor and my wife is a nurse," the man says, looking at Shannon's face. "I hear air, but the obstruction's still there. Don't do the Heimlich yet."

"Why?" I ask.

"What's in there? A piece of meat?" the nurse asks.

"No," I say, the words surreal. "It's an engagement ring."

Shannon looks up, eyes feral. She points to her throat, then to her left hand's ring finger.

I nod.

The nurse looks at Shannon's plate, the glasses on the table, the setting. "It was in the Champagne?"

"No. The tiramisu, apparently."

Sirens wind up in the distance.

Shannon grabs my throat. Her throat labors to get air into her. The doctor checks her other hand, examining her fingernails. She sounds like she's breathing through a straw. Tears pour down her face and she looks half mad.

I did this to her.

Me.

Not a bee.

And no EpiPen is going to fix this.

Then the thin hiss comes to a brutal stop.

The doctor opens her mouth and looks in. "The ring is caught and it's blocking air flow." He holds Shannon's face in his hands, forcing her eyes to look at him. "Cough."

"Unng."

The hissing begins. The sound is like a baby's first cry to my ears. Relief floods me.

Chandra appears and says, "The paramedics are in the building and on their way up."

"How big is the ring?" the doctor asks.

"Three carats."

Two audible whistles come from the other diners.

"I think the ring is caught in such a way that as it moves, she gets some air flow from the band itself," he explains. "The problem is that the ring could cause damage to the esophagus. We need to get her to a hospital immediately."

Shannon's frantic hand finds mine. Her lips are tinged with purple. But she's breathing.

The elevator doors open and clattering in the foyer makes me turn and look. In walks a team of paramedics, one carrying a big tank of oxygen. The doctor visibly relaxes.

His wife rubs Shannon's shoulder. "It'll be okay. You're going to be fine." She looks at me. "Why was the ring in the tiramisu?"

"That is a good question," I growl. "It was supposed to be in the Champagne, where she could see it! Not buried under a bunch of cream and rum-soaked ladyfingers."

Shannon can't even look at me. A paramedic straps an oxygen mask over her head and starts murmuring something to her in calm, dulcet tones. I should be comforting her. I should be fixing this.

I should have never put her in this position in the first place.

Chandra stands by, wringing her hands, and I march over to her. "Why the hell was the ring in her *food*?"

She looks shocked. "Those were your written instructions. The ones Giuseppe gave us! We thought it was unconventional, but you asked that we follow his specifications."

"I never wanted the ring in her tiramisu!"

"Waste of perfectly good tiramisu," some woman's voice says from a distant table.

182

Grace's call about Giuseppe sends a chill down my back. Damn. That must be what this was about.

The paramedics hustle Shannon out to the foyer. I follow, Chandra at my heels and apologizing profusely. I cut her off with a comment that we'll deal with this later, and then Shannon disappears into a crowd of first responders, leaving me to merge my two selves back into one again and follow her to the hospital.

The string quartet appears, the violinist playing the carefully-arranged song "Such Great Heights," the one that reminds me so much of *us*. Her eyes go feral as she watches the tuxedoed string player dip his bow in confusion, his note going flat as the elevator doors close.

Perfect.

Just perfect.

CHAPTER FIFTEEN

The Emergency Room...

"I got your text!" Amanda says in a hushed tone as she pulls back the curtain to Shannon's little room in the ER. The thin hissing sound has been steady now for the past hour, but Shannon's lips and fingernails are a light shade of purple that fills me with unending fear.

"Thanks for coming,"

"She swallowed the ring?" Amanda asks in a tone of voice that somehow manages to bridge incredulity and defeatism. Not many people can pull that off.

"Ung ung ung," Shannon says, giving Amanda raised eyebrows and a sad look. I think she's saying *I am here* but it's hard to tell given her ability to use only one syllable.

"Sorry." Amanda can speak Ring, apparently, and looks at Shannon. "You swallowed it?"

Shannon nods sadly.

"It's seriously stuck in your throat?"

Shannon widens her eyes and manages to say *duh* without saying the word.

"Why on earth would you do this to her!" Amanda says to me savagely.

Here it comes.

"This was never part of the plan, Amanda. The ring was supposed to be in the Champagne."

"How original."

Shannon folds her arms over her chest and she and Amanda share a knowing look.

"The tiramisu was a breakdown in communication."

"How do you get from a ring in a glass to a ring in a layered dessert made of orgasmic perfection?" she asks. Shannon's eyes widen and if she could speak, she'd say, *I know, right?*

"Once we get the ring out of Shannon I'll deal with that. Right now we're more concerned about her oxygenation than on pointing fingers of blame."

Speaking of blame, in walks my brother. "Dude, I cannot believe you get her to swallow and it's a— Oh." He's texting as he talks to me, eyes down, until he looks up and bangs into Amanda's backside.

"Sorry. I—"

They both freeze. He doesn't even look at her, can't even see her face because he's behind her, but he inhales deeply, eyes closing, and says quietly, "Amanda?"

Who knew eyeballs had that much white on them? Amanda's (ample) chest begins to rise and fall like a drunk frat boy playing with a shake weight.

"Andrew," she says in a deadly voice.

My brother turns on his heel and walks right out of the room, head down, pretending to text. Amanda spins around, too, and follows him, calling back, "I'll get Shannon a latte and be back in a minute."

"That was weird," I say to Shannon.

She looks around the bed furtively, then motions to me, pretending to write.

Ah. Pen and paper. I reach for my phone, open a notes app, and hand it to her.

What are those two doing? she types.

"Hell if I know."

Follow them.

"I'd rather drink battery acid than see what they're about to do, Shannon."

Don't make jokes about burning throats, she writes.

Shit.

Does he like her? she types.

"Isn't it obvious?"

Why doesn't he ask her out? she writes.

I take the phone from her, read the question, and then look at her. She's so pale, her face covered with an oxygen mask. She's hissing like Darth Vader and wearing a pulse ox monitor.

"Honey. Shannon," I say, sitting on the bed next to her, careful not to disturb the tubes. "Andrew and Amanda's screwed up relationship really, really shouldn't be the center of your attention right now."

Tears fill her eyes.

"I'm so sorry, baby. I am so, so sorry," I say, finally able to give her the quiet devotion she deserves. "I am an idiot."

She just nods assent.

"A fool."

She agrees.

"A lovesick dumbass."

She purses her lips and tries to sigh. It sounds like a car backfiring.

A commotion in the hallway is punctuated by a shrill woman's voice that says, "I don't care that she's an adult and has privacy protections, I'm her mother and I demand to know where she is!"

Marie.

"Shannon!" she shouts. "Shannon, where are you?"

Fuck, Shannon mouths.

Heard that. Loud and clear.

"We're in here, Marie," I say calmly, pulling the curtain aside.

"My baby!" she gasps, rushing to Shannon, who is wheezing again. "Did you get stung again?"

"Not exactly," I mumble.

Someone in scrubs, wearing a clipboard, comes up behind Marie and—of course—Jason. "You can't just barge in here like this." The hospital official looks at Shannon, who gasps, "S'okay."

"This is her mother," I tell the worker.

"And you are?"

"Her husband."

Marie comes to a dead halt. She could be in a wax museum. "Husband?"

The worker wanders off. Marie gawks at me, then looks at Shannon, who is bent over and focused on getting more oxygen into her. I'd imagine that the stress is going to make breathing that much harder, and start to analyze at what point I need to become a giant asshole in an effort to protect Shannon.

"You got married without *me*?"

Sooner rather than later, apparently.

Amanda appears from behind the curtain, her hair ruffled and lipstick smeared. "Marie?" she says, clearly relieved. "You got my text?"

"We did," Jason says. He's wearing cutoff jeans, flip-flops, and a Jimmy Buffet t-shirt. His knees have actual dirt on them. "Marie came out of the house screaming that Shannon was in the ER again and we jumped in the car as fast as we could."

I take a second look at Marie. She looks like Two-Face, from Batman.

"I was in the middle of my beauty regimen! Jason was about to shower and we were going to see Blue Man Group, when Amanda texted me and I'd only put on one set of eyelashes—"

That explains it.

Marie gives Amanda the once-over. "Why do you have your shirt on inside out?"

Andrew appears at the door and catches my eye. "You need me? Because I'm getting calls from Singapore about the—"

"You would seriously abandon your brother at a time like this?" Amanda snaps at him. "What kind of person are you? Who does that? Shows up for a brief and shining moment and then just bails when it's most important?"

Is Andrew's shirt on backwards?

Wait a minute. What's going on with them?

Before Andrew can answer, in walks a tall, vaguely Slavic-looking guy a few inches taller than me and built like a Russian hockey player, but without the broken cheekbones. And he has all his teeth.

All the women in the room make a sickly sucking sound just like Shannon's breathing.

"Hi, everyone," he announces. He's wearing a white physician's coat and a hospital badge. "I'm Dr.

Derjian, and I'll assess—" he looks at the clipboard at the end of the bed "—Shannon's case."

Jason sticks out his hand to introduce himself. "Jason Jacoby. I'm her father." They shake hands and I realize I need to engage in this masculine ritual that is akin to the female air kiss.

Formality dispensed with, Dr. Derjian examines Shannon's file while Amanda and Marie examine him.

Marie lasers in on him, eyes flitting from his left hand to his face. "You ever see a case like this before, Dr. Derjian? A swallowed engagement ring is pretty out there, isn't it?"

He smiles, a broad, white grin that makes Marie look like she's about to hump his leg. "Oh, this is pretty par for the course when you work in the emergency room. I've seen some pretty strange items in some really weird places."

Marie leans in, grabs his arm and says, "I really need to get to know you better."

"Marie," Jason says with an undertone of warning. "Leave the doctor alone so he can help Shannon."

"Is it true people come into the ER with live animals up their buttholes?" Marie asks.

Dr. Derjian looks at Marie with the same expression I've directed at her hundreds of times over these past eighteen months. *I feel you, bro. Bet your mother-in-law is a lot saner than mine.*

"Marie," Jason says again, this time gently taking her elbow and turning her toward the door. "We've talked about this. Looked it up on Snopes. It doesn't happen. Let's go get some coffee."

190

"But you're already holding a coffee cup in your other hand," she protests. "Wait!"

Shuffling back into the room and giving Shannon a Mother of the Year sympathy smile designed to look good for an audience, she fishes through her purse and hands the doctor a business card.

At this point, it's clear to me that he's decided she's a garden-variety loon. Which makes him right.

"Please. I run a yoga class and we would love to have a fit, eligible bachelor doctor come and visit."

"But I'm not—"

"You don't do yoga? That's okay. That's why it's called a class—you're a student, there to learn." She pats him gently on the cheek, moving her hand down to his arm, testing his biceps with little squeezes followed by satisfied little breaths. "I'll save you a special spot in the front row."

"Watch out for Agnes," I warn him. "She pinches."

"No, I do yoga," he replies as Marie's eyes light up like a set of fireworks in the hands of unsupervised twelve year old boys. He shoots me a very confused look. "But I'm not an eligible bachelor."

"Married?" Marie squeaks, horrified, the light dimming like an imploding dwarf star.

"Engaged," he says.

I'll bet *his* fiancée didn't swallow her ring.

Amy's red, bouncing curls make an appearance. "What's going on? Amanda texted me. Is Shannon all right?" Marie waves her in. The little ER space assigned to Shannon is beginning to feel like a clown car.

Shannon waves her hands like she's trapped on a desert island and we're all search planes. She points to her throat, then the doctor.

He opens her throat and peers in with a flashlight. "Oh, wow."

"Yeah, I know. It's in there tight, isn't it?" I say.

"That's what *she* said," Marie mutters under her breath. Andrew looks murderous. Amy kicks her in the ankle. Beat me to it.

Something old, something new, something borrowed, something stuffed down your future mother-in-law's throat to shut her up...those are the rituals, right?

"Marie," I grunt. She doesn't look at me, but she bites her lips as Jason drags her out of the room, muttering about that coffee.

"Oh." The doctor takes another look. "Yes, it is. I was reacting to the size of that rock." He sizes me up. "Good for you. Makes the ring I proposed with look like a salt crystal."

Shannon starts to say something but the doctor touches her hand and shakes his head. "You can't talk at all. Right now, you're breathing through the ring itself, but any vibration or sudden movement could dislodge it in the worst way possible. You need to stay calm and focused. We're getting equipment right now that will help us to extract the ring."

Equipment? Extract? Panic blooms in Shannon's eyes. My own throat spasms in sympathy. He spends the next minute peering into her throat with the flashlight, hands steady.

"What have we here?" says a clipped women's voice, her British accent as condescending as it was eighteen months ago.

You have got to be kidding me.

Evaluative eyes take in the scene, with Amanda, Amy, me and Shannon all a familiar set of characters to her. "Dr. Porter." She frowns at Shannon, then looks at me. "You two? I remember you." She points to Shannon. "Bee sting." Then to me. "EpiPen to the groin." She pauses, the incredulity rising in her voice like a tidal wave. "Again? Did she actually touch your penis this time, or was it a false alarm?"

Andrew gives me one of those looks that means I'll never hear the end of this. Ever.

Marie and Jason walk back in as the doctor asks us, "What is it with you two? Do you have some sort of dating fetish that involves coming to the ER?" The words feel harsher in that British accent of hers, and women with grey hair and glasses always have the upper hand when it comes to judgmental comments. If my mother were still alive, I wonder what she would think of this mess.

If Mom were alive, her ring wouldn't be caught in Shannon's throat right now.

"Is that a real thing? An ER fetish?" Marie asks, breathless with possibility. "I'm kind of an expert on fetishes."

Dr. Porter gives her a withering look and turns to Shannon. "Your mother, right?"

Shannon nods.

"The fetish thing makes more sense." Dr. Porter's eyebrows are doing a judgmental dance but she stops talking to us and reads the chart.

"Seriously? I'd love to know. I work in the sex industry." Marie announces this with a series of nods designed, I think, to convey her professional status as...a *what*?

Jason begins sputtering. "You do not work in the sex industry, Marie! Why on earth would you say such a thing?"

"I mystery shop sex toy stores!" Marie declares. "I'm a professional!"

"*So* not the same thing, Mom," Amy says with a sigh. "We've been trying to explain this to her," she says to the room in a resigned voice. "She doesn't get it. She's been telling everyone around town, at church, at the library, you name it, that she works in the sex industry."

"Now everyone in town thinks my wife is a hooker!" Jason declares, looking angrier than I've ever seen him. Even angrier than the time he confronted me after I dumped Shannon. While I like Jason and we bond over good beer in his little shack in the backyard, he's a beta. The kind of guy, like Greg, who lets women drag them around by the nose.

Shannon will never do that to me. There are *other* body parts I'll let her drag me around by, but—

"Only when we role play, Jason," Marie says with a sigh.

"How did the ring get in there?" Dr. Porter asks the question with a suggestive tone that I don't like.

Marie, Jason, Amy, Andrew and Amanda all turn to me with looks of expectation on their face. "Good question," Andrew says slowly. "You haven't told us that part yet."

194

Shannon starts to make gagging noises and points to her throat.

Marie's eyes fly wide open. "Oh. Oh, honey," she says, patting Shannon's hand. "You know they make special sex toys just for that. You don't have to put that kind of ring around a man and then put your mouth, you know..."

The meaning of her words hits me like a two-by-four. Both doctors are looking at us like this is a plausible explanation for how Shannon came to have the ring stuck in her throat. From the look on Shannon's face, she's as horrified as I am.

For a completely different reason.

"Let me set the record straight!" I say with an angry hiss. "We did not put my *mother's* engagement ring over my..." I gesture toward my groin, "and then have her..." I gesture toward Shannon's mouth.

Andrew turns beet red. "Hold on! That's *Mom's* ring?"

Shit. Caught.

"It's okay, Declan," Marie says softly. "People experiment."

"The ring would never fit," I snap.

Dr. Porter cocks a skeptical eyebrow. Dr. Derjian, good man that he is, stays silent and his face is as neutral as a football ref's. "Flaccid, yes," Dr. Porter explains. "The ring could slide down and—"

"You would need a bracelet," I explain, standing as tall as possible, "not a piddly little engagement ring."

Marie looks at Shannon. "You lucky girl."

"You lucky bastard," Jason mutters.

"Who said you could have Mom's ring?" Andrew bellows.

"Anyhow, that's not how Shannon ate the ring," I continue, completely ignoring him. "She took a bite of tiramisu and swallowed it."

"Who puts a three carat diamond ring in tiramisu?" Andrew asks.

"Yeah?" Marie demands. "Why ruin good tiramisu like that?"

I really don't get the female obsession with this dessert.

Marie's face pauses as she starts to speak again. She shakes her head slightly, as if in shock. "Three carats? *Three carats?*"

I just smile.

"Lucky bastard," Jason says again.

Dr. Derjian and Dr. Porter have these long devices that look like tweezers on steroids. I can see Shannon's heart throbbing in terror against her ribcage. The room starts to spin, and I can inhale as much air as I need. She can't.

Marie sidles her way over to Shannon and takes her hand. "He proposed?"

Shannon shakes her head.

Marie's eyes flash like Godzilla laser eyes on me. "You made her eat a three carat engagement ring and never even bothered to ask her to marry you? Is that some ethnic ritual from your people?"

My people?

"My people are Scottish, Marie. My people don't eat engagement rings. It's a complicated story."

"It better be a complicated story if it involves having a rock like that caught in her throat!"

196

Everyone looks at me. They all seem to be waiting for an explanation.

Time to give them one.

"I'll say this once: I hired Greg to pretend to beg Shannon to do a mystery shop at Le Portmanteau."

Shannon's eyes turn Godzilla-like, too.

"I arranged with the staff to have my mom's engagement ring put in a glass of Champagne."

Dr. Porter and Dr. Derjian share raised eyebrows. "Classic," he says to her.

Marie starts to say something and I hold up a finger. "The staff screwed up and put the ring in the tiramisu instead of the Champagne."

"Who ruins tiramisu like that?" Dr. Porter muses.

All the women in the room nod.

"Shannon took a bite and here we are."

No one says a word. Everyone just blinks.

"That's it?" Marie finally pipes up, indignant. "Oh, please." She pulls back from Shannon, leans her forward a bit, and hauls off and whacks her so hard it sounds like a loud clap.

"NO!" the doctors shout in unison.

A weird gagging noise comes out of Shannon, then a great big whoop of breath.

"MOM!"

"MARIE!"

"HOLY SHIT!"

"I swallowed it," Shannon says in a tinny voice. A round of coughing makes her bark like a seal, then sigh.

Andrew and Amanda come running back in.

"I can breathe," Shannon explains. "But I feel like there's a basketball caught in my chest."

"Do you have any idea how dangerous that was?" Dr. Porter's voice is murderous steel, her finger in Marie's face. "What on earth were you thinking?" Dr. Derjian opens Shannon's mouth again and looks in, examining.

Marie gives her a condescending look. "I am the mother of three girls and the grandmother to two boys. A good whack on the back is all anyone with something lodged in their throat needs." She looks at Shannon with an exaggerated expression of patience and holds out her hand. "Spit it out."

"I said I swallowed it, Mom."

"No one swallows a -- what?" Marie gasps.

"Your arrogance will kill someone," Dr. Porter shoots back, making Marie go white. Her confidence is gone.

"Mild lacerations and significant swelling," Dr. Derjian says evenly, examining Shannon's throat again. He's clearly pissed at Marie, too. "What's the metal?"

"Platinum," I say.

"Good," he adds, nodding. "No worries about allergies."

"She's allergic to bees," Marie says in a small voice.

"I mean metal allergies," he clarifies.

"What now?" Shannon croaks out.

"Water. Cool water," Dr. Derjian says, turning to pour her some. "Sip slowly, through the straw. We'll have to order X-rays now." Dr. Porter glares at Marie but nods.

"As long as the ring doesn't get stuck, the only way out is through," he says with a mild smile.

"Through?" Jason asks.

Derjian cocks an eyebrow. "Through."

Andrew chooses this moment to speak. "When you say 'through', you mean..."

"It has to be pooped out," Marie whispers.

The two doctors nod.

"Let's not get ahead of ourselves," Dr. Porter says. "We need to get visual confirmation that it's in the esophagus, that it's not perforating, and to make certain it continues to move through the digestive tract properly."

"I have to poop my own engagement ring out," Shannon says, then clutches her throat, pounding on her chest. She looks remarkably like a mama gorilla.

"Can't you just crack her chest open and do surgery?" Marie asks, mortified.

Shannon nods vigorously. "Please," she whispers. "That would be so much better."

"Don't talk," Dr. Porter orders. She opens Shannon's mouth and peers in. "The swelling may get worse before it gets better. Drink the cool water and don't speak for a few hours."

"Maybe I should have you swallow a ring if it meant a doctor ordered *you* not to speak for a few hours," Jason says to Marie.

"I'm sorry!" Marie says to Shannon.

"S'okay."

"Don't speak!" I remind her.

Shannon nods, motioning for my phone. I give it to her, but she's shaking, tears pouring out of her eyes.

"She has to poop the ring out," Andrew says again. He's not just Captain Obvious, he's the CEO of Obvious, Inc.

"Yes," the doctors say. "Most likely," Dr. Porter clarifies.

Andrew looks at me. "You can totally have that ring, bro."

"No shit," I say.

"Um, actually, *yes* shit," Amanda notes.

We all groan. Except for Shannon, who just weeps quietly and pokes at my phone. She finally holds it up and I read:

I'm sorry I swallowed your mother's ring.

It's like a gut punch.

I type back: *I'm sorry I ruined your tiramisu.*

She reads it and gives me a choking laugh, plus a look with eyes filled with love and the future. It's the first genuine moment we've had all day, the only moment not fraught with irritation or disaster, and all I want to do is clear the room and take her in my arms.

"Congratulations," Andrew says, shaking my hand.

"She hasn't said yes," I point out.

"You haven't even proposed yet!" Shannon growls.

"Shhhh!" Marie and Jason say to her.

"She *can't* say yes," he replies. "Literally."

I try to hide my smile. "You'll be my best man?"

"Sure."

"Farmington Country Club?" Amanda asks, looking at Shannon, who just shrugs.

Marie bursts out with, "Yes! An outdoor wedding!"

"I take it back," Andrew mutters. "Terry will be a good choice."

Amanda whacks him in the shoulder. "You are such a jerk! Get over your stupid phobia about being outdoors! You seriously would refuse to..."

He holds his palms up in surrender and leaves. Amanda follows him, berating him. Their arguing voices fade as they get farther away. I'll deal with my stupid jerk phobic brother later. Right now I have a ring-filled, not-quite fiancée who has to give birth to her own engagement ring. Through her butthole.

A medical assistant walks in with an assortment of supplies, but the most noteworthy item in her hands is a giant stack of empty French fry trays. The red-and-white patterned kind.

"What are those?" I ask.

She looks at me and smiles, so chipper she could be a punk cheerleader. Long blue hair in pigtails. Bright blue eyes. She has a bandage over a tattoo and a hole in her lip where a piercing obviously normally goes. Braces. She looks young enough for Dad to date.

"Oh, that's to catch the ring!"

"The—"

"You'll use those when you eliminate, Shannon," Dr. Porter says to her. "Felicia here will give you a list of foods that will help speed up the process." She pauses. "And tiramisu is not one of them."

"Then you assume this is the best course of treatment," I ask. Marie, Jason and Amy have fallen silent, jaws slightly open, minds blown like mine.

Dr. Porter looks at Shannon's chart, hooks it to the end of the bed, and pats her foot, speaking directly to Shannon. "Let's get you into X-ray and go from there, but most of the time just eliminating the foreign object and letting the digestive tract do its job is the least invasive course."

"You are going to shit diamonds," Amy says to Shannon. She starts to clap.

"A gold brick," Marie adds with a knowing grin.

"Platinum." My correction goes unnoticed. I'm imagining Andrew right now, texting Dad, and the laugh they're about to have about this.

It's not like dropping a phone in the toilet.

"This will be the most expensive poop in history," Jason adds.

"Diamonds are forever," Amy jokes. "Until you eat the prunes."

The medical assistant, Felicia, picks up the French fry trays and an instruction sheet. "So, Shannon," she starts.

Marie interrupts her. "Brings a whole new meaning to the phrase, 'You want fries with that?'"

I look at Marie, who starts to giggle. Jason joins in, followed by Amy. While it's funny—it really is, on the face of it—the look of pure, unadulterated horror on Shannon's face makes me realize my place in this world.

Time to be the asshole.

"Get out," I demand, the words booming in the room, as if my voice is the only sound that matters.

And it is.

"You can't make us just—"

I cut Marie off. "Yes. I can." Amy, Marie and Jason stand their ground.

"Shannon's a grown woman who can—"

"Shannon is a weeping pile of gorgeousness who is traumatized by swallowing the ring and now doubly traumatized by having a Keystone Kops family humiliating her, so you all need to leave!"

My lovely future wife gives me a grateful look.

Marie shoots Jason a look that might as well say *Show your balls.*

He opens his mouth and says, "Declan, I know this is upsetting, and you feel guilty for being so reckless with your mother's ring, but—"

"OUT!"

He flinches. Marie just gets angrier.

The medical assistant now checking Shannon's oxygen stats hands gives me a thumbs up.

"Look here," Marie blusters. "I know you think you're this dominant—"

That's it. I move swiftly, my blood on fire. Shannon's crying, Dr. Derjian is rubbing her shoulder, and the jokes are out of control. Amy gets to the threshold and hovers.

All that's left are Marie and Jason.

"I am Shannon's husband," I declare.

"Not yet," Marie hisses. "And I'm her mother, and I need to make sure she's okay."

"You are all that's left that is making her *not* okay."

She looks like I slapped her.

"Once we're married, I'm her legal next of kin," I stress. There is no way they're winning this one. *Tough shit, lady. I love you and your crazy family and your wonderful daughter, but I have had it up to here.*

And *here*, ironically, is where the ring got stuck in Shannon.

"You're not married yet."

"We can fix that easily within twenty-four hours."

Marie is horrified. "You wouldn't."

"Try me."

Jason cocks one eyebrow.

Shannon looks at him, then her mother, and just nods, pointing to the door.

"You wouldn't really just go to the courthouse and get married, would you? Without me there? Without the flowers and the dress and the cake and the helicopter and the President and—"

At some point Shannon gets her hands on a notepad and a pen. She scribbles furiously and holds it up.

It says:

VEGAS

"Noooooooooooo!" Marie moans.

"Todd and Carol may have been onto something," I say.

Jason's silent, just watching us all, eyebrows turned in with concern as he settles on Shannon. I look at her and she reaches for my hand.

"I want to be alone," she rasps. "With Declan."

"But—"

Jason slides his arm around Marie's waist and turns her, like a square dancer. Allemande left and out the door....

"Let's go, Marie."

"He can't just—"

"Yes, he can. He just did."

She turns around and gives us both a red-rimmed look with pleading eyes. "Don't really run off to Vegas. Can you imagine if you pooped that ring out in a public toilet in a casino? You would—"

I cross the room and yank the curtain closed. It's not nearly as satisfying as slamming a door. Too bad there's no lock.

Shannon sags against the bed, her entire body relaxing.

"Thank you."

"Don't talk. No need to thank me. It's my job now."

"But you were kind of an asshole."

I blink. "Excuse me?"

She motions for my phone and types:

Remember how you're supposed to think about other people's feelings before you pound your chest and call yourself silverback?

My jaw could shovel sidewalks.

"You're making *me* the bad guy here? They were being jerks to you."

That's just how they are, she types. *They joke because they love me. They're family.*

"Then I don't know how to *family*!"

"What?" she gasps.

"You heard me. I have no idea how to do this family thing."

205

"No, no," she rasps. "I heard you. I understand. I just can't believe you turned the word 'family' into a verb."

I stare at her. *That's* what she got out of what I said? That I broke a grammar rule?

"I don't know if I can be with a man who turns nouns into verbs. I just can't *even*!" She starts to laugh, then gags a little. I pour her a cup of water and add some crushed ice, then sit on the bed next to her, urging her to drink. The cold water should reduce the swelling.

She sips slowly through the straw, then says, "I am the worst person for you to pick as your wife."

"Stop talking! And I'll be the judge of that."

"You can withdraw your offer."

"My offer? This isn't a merger, Shannon. It's a proposal. Or, at least, it will be once we get the ring back. For marriage. And love." I frown. "Unless you want me to withdraw..."

The world as I know it becomes a frozen void. Time is meaningless. Space is optional. Molecules don't have purpose.

She shakes her head no, and life resumes. "Don't withdraw. But don't be so mean."

I sit down and hold her hands, capturing her eyes. "I love you, Shannon. More than I think even I realize. And when people—even your parents—make you suffer, it makes me crazy. They push your bounds and my buttons and I'm not putting up with it. I'm just not. You have to understand that." We're in dangerous territory now.

"And," she rasps, pausing to take a sip, "you're the kind of man who needs a woman who doesn't flush her phone or swallow heirlooms." Sip. "Or nearly die from a bee sting."

"That was entirely my fault."

"You can't claim responsibility for all of those. But I'll blame you for the spiked tiramisu."

I close my eyes and groan, squeezing her hand.

"I mean, really." Sip. "Who's stupid enough to have a symbol of your undying love tucked away in a piece of food that is the female equivalent of—" She starts coughing and can't stop, the rest of her sentence lost to the ravages of metal and diamond making its way through her organs.

A guy in scrubs appears at the door. "Shannon Jacoby? I'm here to take you to X-ray."

For the next hour I sit in an uncomfortable chair and text with Grace nonstop, trying to figure out where this all went wrong. At some point I nod off.

When I wake up with a neck cramp and a phone out of battery Shannon's back, dozing in the bed, propped up.

"Dec?" she whispers. I jump up, disoriented. I fell asleep? I don't take naps unless I'm naked and Shannon's with me, and those naps don't involve any actual sleep. Unreal.

"You need something?" I ask.

"I just need to know—" She coughs, the sound a weird rattle in her bones.

Dr. Derjian walks in, frowning. Our discussion has to be tabled, and Shannon's eyes are troubled. I imagine mine don't look too happy, either. He grabs his stethoscope and holds it up to her chest, listening intently as her coughs recede.

"We got the X-rays," he declares, unsheathing them from a large manila envelope. He holds one up to the fluorescent light. Shannon and I look up, as if we're stargazing.

The ring is an obvious object, right smack in the middle of her chest, embedded under her ribs.

"Ouch," she says.

"Ouch," Dr. Derjian and I agree.

"Do I need surgery?" she asks. Her face is hopeful. She really would rather have her chest sawed open than the alternative.

The doctor points to the stack of French fry trays he and Dr. Porter gave her earlier. "Not yet. Those should be the best medical tools, in the end."

My inner twelve year old wants to snicker. He said *In the end*.

Shannon gives me a sharp look, as if she read my mind. "So I just have to wait it out?"

He nods. "Prune juice, apricot nectar, lots of high-fiber foods. Leafy greens. Felicia has a list of suggested foods."

Mom's ring stares at us, a white object in stark relief against Shannon's inner workings.

"It won't rip her as it goes through?" I ask.

Steady, dark brown eyes meet mine. He's sharp and calm. "It shouldn't, but any sharp abdominal pain needs to be met with an immediate trip to the ER."

"Do you know Dr. Porter's schedule?" Shannon asks.

He cocks one eyebrow. "Any attending physician will be very competent in treating you."

She waves her hand. "No. I want to know when she's working so I can *avoid* her. If I want to be judged with snooty haughtiness I'll go find my ex's mom and ask her opinion on my fashion choices."

"Stop talking," Dr. Derjian and I say together.

He gives me a look and I ask, "They can't help themselves, can they? Your fiancée's a talker?'

A flash of three or four different emotions pass through his face before he replies, "You could say that."

The look we give each other seems to say, *I share your pain, bro.*

He finishes some notes on Shannon's chart and looks up at her. "The discharge nurse will be in shortly with instructions."

"That's it?" I ask, adrenaline seeping out of my pores, exhaustion filling me.

"For now." He pats Shannon's knee. "Just come in for any pains you encounter."

She points to me. "Does that include him?" Dr. Derjian laughs and leaves the room.

Amanda comes rushing back. "I can take Shannon home." She cocks an eyebrow and seems to watch the doctor walk down the hall. "Take him home, too, if he's single..."

Andrew better make his move. Fast.

"I want her to come back to my place."

Shannon shakes her head "no" with such violence I think she's make the ring come flying out of her.

"What?" Alarm and confusion fill me. "Why not?" There's no better place for her to recover than with me.

209

She and Amanda look at me like I'm the stupidest person on earth. Shannon points to the French fry trays.

"Declan, do you seriously think there is any person alive who wants to hang out with their beloved while they wait to shit out their engagement ring?" Amanda asks. Shannon just buries her face in a spare pillow.

"When you put it that way..."

"Think of it like a colonoscopy."

"What?"

"You ever take your dad to the hospital for his routine colonoscopy?"

"No. My father barely has time for a handshake. We don't take each other to places where we have someone shove things in our asses."

She gives me a hairy look. "You're just like your brother."

I'm not sure whether to be offended or pleased.

"My point," she continues, "is that no one wants to be watched while they have things coming out of their butt that might be embarrassing."

Which is every object that was ever up there, right?

"I see." And I do. I guess if Shannon has to go through the unbearable humiliation of shitting out her own engagement ring, the only thing that could make it worse is to have me there.

"I am never, ever eating French fries again," Shannon mumbles from behind her pillow.

A quick kiss on her cheek and a look of assurance from Amanda and I head out, wondering how I went from the perfect proposal to the perfect disaster.

And I still haven't even popped the question.

CHAPTER SIXTEEN

Poopwatch, Day 1...

Andrew's phone call comes out of nowhere the next morning. Shannon's at her apartment, refusing to see me until the ring comes out, busy eating bran cereal and prunes. That tiny little place is going to smell like a frat house soon.

"You see Jessica's tweet?" Andrew's voice has a triumphant tone that sets my competitive streak to Engage.

"I unfollowed her a long time ago, bro." Grace hasn't given me a report today. What's this about?

"You might want to check it out, because Shannon's going to lose it when she sees what Jessica's up to."

Remember back in the good old days, in 2010 when Twitter wasn't a topic of conversation? Yeah. Me too. I liked it better when My Space was the in thing and we didn't check in on Facebook to notify people which bathroom we were using in which restaurant.

My phone buzzes with a text.

"That's Shannon," I say. "Thanks for the heads' up."

"Welcome. And let me know how Poopwatch is going."

"What?"

"Poopwatch. That's what Jessica's calling it. Hashtag and all."

"Wait!" Poopwatch? My proposal has a *hashtag*? At least it's not Poopgate. Why does everything have to end in -gate?

Bzzzzz.

"How in the hell did she find out?" I know Shannon's texting me like mad, and I steel myself for the inevitable screeching.

He snorts. "No idea, but it's all over the Twitterverse."

The fact that we have something called "the Twitterverse" is an abomination against nature.

Shannon's text is a screenshot of a tweet from Jessica @jesscoffN. It is a picture of Shannon's x-ray with the ring in sharp contrast to her ribs and soft organs, with the following tweet:

> *Shitty proposal #poopwatch*
> @anterdec2

Next text from Shannon:

> *Can you marry me in jail? Because I'm going to kill her. Just get me a good lawyer if you want conjugal visits.*

I have no doubt about Shannon's homicidal tendencies right now. I have to confess to a touch of Schadenfreude, though, because it's nice to be the one watching her anger instead of being the object of it.

I miss you, I text back.

See you in a few days, she replies.

214

Days? I have to wait days?

No. No wait. I'm coming over today.

You come over today and I let my mother plan your bachelor party, Shannon texts back.

Well, she's got me there. I'm marrying a negotiation shark.

How about you call me when you're ready to see me, I text.

How about I call you to help me bury Jessica's body?

She's only half joking. That's the scary part.

How in the hell did Jessica get her hands on those X-rays? I'm puzzling through that one, madly texting Grace to get her on the job. Ten minutes later someone's at my door. It's Andrew, carrying a bag of bagels and wearing a scowl. The bagel bag slams against my wood counter and he heads straight for my coffeemaker.

"Got any scotch?" He pours himself half a cup of coffee, finds the alcohol before I can answer, and fills the rest of the mug with spirits.

"Help yourself."

"Fucking Amanda."

"You are?"

"No," he says, so upset he's shaking. Either that, or he's such an alcoholic that *delirium tremens* have kicked in. Given his youth and overall vitality, I think it's the former.

"What was going on between you two at the hospital?"

His ears turn pink and he chugs the entire mug of abominable coffee in one big gulp.

"That bad?"

"That *good.*"

"That's worth pursuing."

"That needs to be forgotten."

"Why?"

He looks at me like I have two heads. "Why? When did you start asking all these touchy-feely questions? Because. That's why. *Because.*"

"You sound like Dad."

"I take that as a compliment. Dad's good at compartmentalizing. Great at business. Has a healthy relationship with the ladies."

"He dates zygotes."

"At least zygotes can't talk."

"Jesus, Andrew, why all the anger? Why don't you just sit down with Amanda and have a mature conversation about whatever conflicts you have?"

He frowns and looks me up and down. "You grow a new X chromosome I don't know about? Where's this coming from?"

I cross my arms and lean against the counter, drinking my non-alcoholic coffee. "Nothing wrong with talking about feelings. Real men can do it, too."

"Real men don't have feelings. We have penises with needs. That's our version of emotions."

"Oh, you must really win over the ladies with lines like that."

"My bed's warm enough."

"Could be warmer with Amanda in it."

Pink ears. "Shut up."

"Fine. I'll shut up. Let's talk about making me CEO, then."

He makes a nasty sound in the back of his throat. "Dad would never, ever consider it. Besides, I'd fight you for it. And win."

I look at him. Really look at him.

He's terrified.

And he's right. He would fight me for it and win. Not because I wouldn't be the natural successor to Anterdec after Dad retires (which is his euphemism for *dies*).

But because I want something more than what Dad and Andrew have in their life. Being a CEO isn't part of that *more*.

Terror is what happens to people who start to let their inner selves shine through. Who let themselves hope. Who open themselves to the possibility that real, raw, dirty, messy love is out there and that it's worth it.

Andrew's scared shitless, and he should be.

The day Shannon walked into that meeting eighteen months ago and Toilet Girl turned out to be real I was scared shitless, too.

And that's exactly why I pursued her.

Business challenges involve the thrill of the chase. The brute negotiations where power in the form of money changes hands. The merger of two businesses, the acquisition of a smaller company by a larger entity, and the give and take of oneupmanship that defines the capitalist system.

I'm good at those power struggles. Andrew is great at them. Dad's the king of it all.

Not my kingdom, though.

Toilet Girl shocked me to the core that day in the bathroom, self-effacing and visceral. Stunningly self-deprecating and yet defiant. Shannon went toe to toe with me verbally and was so...something. If I knew the words I'd use them.

"You're right," I say, acquiescing. I know when to stop the tug of war and just let go. "I don't want it."

"Bullshit."

"I have something better."

"Shannon is better than being the CEO of a Fortune 500 company?" he asks, earnest and genuine. No snark. He's trying to understand.

I pause, blinking a few times. But I don't wait too long.

"Yes."

"Why?"

Now who's getting all touchy-feely?

A carefully-constructed case with facts and judgments, analyses and explanations, builds in my mind like a tower. Like scaffolding. Like a court case designed to defend my premise.

But you can't do that with love.

And I don't have to validate my own feelings.

"Why?" I echo him. "Why?"

He nods.

"Because."

He gives me a grimace and a glare. Mom shines through in him just then. It's surreal.

"You'd give up fame and fortune and power for love? How cute."

"No. The great part is that I don't have to give up love for anything."

And with that I go back to texting Grace, ignoring my little brother as he makes himself his

218

second cup of whatever it takes to get him through the day.

Poopwatch, Day 2...

Shannon takes the day off and refuses to text with me. She says it's bad luck to see the groom before you poop out the engagement ring. An old tradition carefully noted in the Emily Post Guide to Modern Weddings.

I work out with Andrew. A lot.

Poopwatch, Day 3...

The closest thing to intimacy with another person I achieve today is the moment Grace's fingers brush against mine while she hands me my morning coffee. Shannon won't talk to me, won't text with me, won't acknowledge my existence. She's taken another day off work and I'm burying myself in projects that don't matter.

Meanwhile, Grace works hard at arranging The Proposal 2.0. The day passes in a blur of meetings and the tedium of waiting for something I have no control over.

Jason appears at my office long after all the staff have gone home for the night. The cleaning crew has taken over the floor, men wearing jetpack vacuums and women carefully sanitizing phones as I hear and knock on my door, the kind of *rap rap rap* that comes after a person has tried repeatedly to get your attention.

I open the door to find Shannon's father standing there, a neutrally friendly look on his face.

"May I come in? I realize I should have called, but this wasn't a planned visit."

I rub the back of my neck and motion for him to come in. He walks with a steady, comfortable gait, attired in his standard jeans and casual shirt. He hasn't shaved in days.

A quick rub of my palm against my own cheek tells me I probably look a little grubby, too.

"A drink?" I ask. "I've got Scotch." Shannon told me long ago it's his favorite second only to local microbrewed beer.

His eyes flash with mischief. "Sounds great."

I hand him two fingers, neat.

"You pay attention," he says slowly.

I shrug, then slam my own drink down like a shot of tequila at an all-night poker game in Vegas. Normally, I'd never drink while burning the midnight oil like this, but something about Jason makes me think it's not a bad idea to loosen up a bit.

He follows my lead, then sets the glass down on my desk and walks to the window. City lights dot the ground like an inverse blanket of stars.

"Helluva view," he says with a longing sigh.

Nodding, I just smile. "It is."

"You've grown up with this." A tone of marvel fills his words.

"Yes." Why argue? He's right.

"But your dad didn't." Jason runs a hand through his thinning hair. "He may have married into money, but he wasn't born into it. That's for sure. I remember James. Smart as hell and determined."

"You knew him?"

"Only because of Marie," Jason says, looking at me with eyes so similar to Shannon's I have to check myself and remember they're not attached to her. "She kept bringing these injured animals to the vet where I worked back then, and one night she brought James in. You'd have thought she'd asked him to eat dinner at the garbage dump." He laughs. "And yet he found a way to pay for every injured animal. That was right before he hit it big."

"Before he met my mom."

Jason frowns. "Your mom. Marie told me about your talk at the cemetery."

Of course she did.

I stay silent, wondering if I should pour us another round.

"Your mom's from Mayflower people, right?"

I nod.

"And old money."

My body goes tight. Where is this conversation heading.

"Yes."

"She helped James, didn't she?"

"With investments? Sure. My grandfather did." That's all public record.

"You've grown up with all this wealth your entire life, then."

"Yes."

"But James...James is all Southie."

"Jason," I ask slowly, fighting back a defensive tone, "why are you here?"

He gives a wan smile. "It's about Shannon and the hospital incident."

"Which one?"

He chuckles, then shakes his head. "My girls and their mother are one of a kind, that's for sure. How many men can ask what you just asked?"

A smile stretches my mouth before I can stop it. "We're lucky."

"Either that, Declan, or we're just stupid and don't realize it."

"Speak for yourself."

We stand and stare out at the city until he says, "You kicked us out of Shannon's room."

"Yes. And with good reason."

He nods and grimaces at the same time. "Marie's awfully hurt."

"So was Shannon. And Shannon's my priority."

"She's ours, too."

"Wouldn't know it back there."

He clears his throat, tongue rolling between his teeth and lips. "You're fairly new to Shannon's life. The jokes are how we all handle stress."

"Doesn't make it okay." This moment is crucial. Thirty years from now, I'll reflect back on it and if I don't make the right choice right here, right now, I'll regret it.

I'm not a man with many regrets. Not adding one right now.

"That doesn't mean you should have ordered us out."

"You could have fought me." I want to ask why he didn't, but the answer might be too raw. Baring my soul to Shannon is hard enough. Opening myself up to Marie at the cemetery was a surprise. Hell if I'm going to be soft and fluffy with Jason over this issue.

If I can't do it, I won't ask another man to do it, either.

He pauses, carefully considering his words. That's one quality I like in Jason. Unlike Marie, who rushes to fill in silence, Jason is comfortable with it. He can take his time before he says what needs to be said.

"I certainly could have. Legally, we had the right to boot you out of that room. We're still Shannon's next of kin."

"But you didn't." *Because I was right*, I want to add.

"No. It was clear that Shannon wanted you to defend her like that, and even if Marie couldn't understand that, I could."

"Marie could have seriously hurt her with that back-smacking stunt," I growl, showing more emotion than I want to.

"I know. She knows it, too. She's back home kicking herself and falling into a shame spiral that no amount of Netflix and pampering can pull her out of."

Shame spiral? These people read too many self-help books.

"But that's not why you made us leave, and you know it."

"Why do you think I made you leave?"

"Because you care more about Shannon's feelings than ours."

Zing.

"Right."

"Which is fine," he adds, searching the room for his glass. He walks over to my desk and picks it up, shaking it in the air. "Got more?"

Relief floods me. I not only have more, I *need* more. Two generous glass refills later and we're back at the window.

He drinks half his tumbler and looks out at the inky night, words aimed at me, eyes aimed up at the stars we can't see.

"Which is fine," he continues, as if we never paused. "But at some point you have to realize Shannon is part of a family, and that eventually all the family members do need to be considered."

"How can I not realize that? It's shoved in my face every day. My penis—excuse me, *penith*—has been made fun of by a child born in the twenty-first century and you and my father engaged in a version of wrestling banned for its eroticism in seventeen countries. At my work. And don't even get me started on Marie..."

I swig the rest of my Scotch and give him a narrow look. "You think I don't understand I'm not just marrying Shannon? That you're all a package deal?"

Jason blinks, eyes tired but steady. "It's like that, huh?" He sighs. It's a sound of disappointment that makes my stomach clench. "You're just going to do what you do and we'll do what we do and it's going to be a mess."

That's the most plainspoken description of my interactions with Shannon's family I've ever heard.

"Yes."

"As long as you always put Shannon first, I'm fine with that." He offers me his hand. I shake it.

"Yes, sir."

He steps back and walks with purpose to the door to my office, ready to leave. I watch him go, mind spinning from trying to understand why he's here and, probably, a little from the Scotch.

"Declan?" he adds right before he walks out. He's smiling, eyes friendly and sharp.

"Yes?"

"Make sure you understand that I'll always put Marie first when you two clash. Just so we're clear."

And with that, he's gone.

Poopwatch, Day 4...

"Auntie Shannon pooped! She pooped!" My phone crackles with an excited eight year old's voice as I answer a call from what I thought was Shannon.

"Poopy! See poopy in da fesh fy tay!" chants Tyler in the background. I'm hoping "See" is his version of "She," because the alternative is just too gross.

"She got the ring, Declan!" Jeffrey crows. "You can be my uncle now. Uncleth give good presents to their nephew, right? And you're rich. I want an X-Box K'nect with—"

Shannon's voice appears, dripping through my ears like honey. "Sorry about that," she laughs. "Jeffrey got a little too excited and knows exactly how to use my phone."

"See? I was right."

"Huh?"

"Little boys love to talk about poop."

She makes a sound of disgust, but hey, she's got to admit I'm right.

"You got the ring?" I ask.

"Yes."

Thank God. Poopwatch 2015 is over.

"Everything okay?"

She snorts. "My mom brought me a bunch of chocolates yesterday. Turns out they had a little something special in them."

"Xanax?"

"Laxatives."

"Ouch."

"Right. I needed an epidural to—oh, why am I talking about this with you?" she screeches, her voice changing from casual closeness to horrified harpy in the blink of an eye.

"You can talk about anything with me, Shannon. I miss you."

"I promise," she says in a rush of urgency, "that we're having your mom's ring cleaned. Sterilized. In fact, we've arranged to have a nuclear bomb detonated so close to it any living organisms will be killed. That should ensure it's truly spic 'n span."

I chuckle and then have no idea what to say. I don't even clean my own underwear, so how would I know what you do in a case like this?

"I can have Grace arrange everything," I tell her. "It's the least I could do."

"Declan, when we have kids someday and I'm not around and a diaper needs to be changed, you know you can't call Grace."

Kids. She mentioned *kids*.

"That's what nannies are for."

"Nannies? More than one?"

"Of course. Three of them in round the clock shifts."

"You're joking." Her voice drops to a register that tells that even if I weren't joking, I have to pretend I am.

"Yes, I am. But not about the diaper part."

Her voice goes soft. "Dec?"

"Yeah?"

"We need to talk."

My chest tightens. "We do?"

"Well, there's this ring here, and...."

"About that," I say with a smile. "What are you doing tomorrow?"

"Throwing all my French fry trays away."

"After that?"

"Going to work."

"How about a helicopter ride?"

"To the lighthouse?"

"No. Somewhere better."

Somewhere *perfect*.

CHAPTER SEVENTEEN

The Proposal 2.0...

Marie's helicopter envy is understandable when you look at cities from the standpoint of having to get around in them. Landing at the Anterdec helipad is a breeze compared to trucking into the city from JFK or LaGuardia, limo or no limo.

Anterdec's New York City driver, Sam, takes our bags and delivers them to our corporate suite at the company's finest hotel in Manhattan.

"Where is he taking my bag?" Shannon shouts over the sound of the copter.

"To the hotel."

"Aren't we going there?" she asks, looking at me with curiosity.

"Not yet." First things first.

Shannon is remarkably silent on the limo ride to our destination, giving me half smiles and little caresses. Sex in the limo in a new city is a bit daunting, and for once I don't want to sleep with her.

I know, I know. Back up the limo. That's right.

I *don't* want to sleep with her. Not now.

I'm too wound up, too full of cortisol and adrenaline and testosterone and whatever hormones drive me to ask her to marry me. My cup runneth over and I'm both full and empty, both free and chained. Cupid's arrow struck me but it was attached to a rope that binds me to Shannon. We're tied to each other for eternity.

The proposal is just a formality.

"How can you get away from work like this?" she asks, as if the thought suddenly came to her. "Isn't the New Zealand launch a big mess? How can you take two days off?"

I give her a puffed-up, proud smile. "Got it all under control. Dad handed me that big mess but with the right management, I got new subcontractors in on the development, a crack software support team, and we sent coupon codes out to sixteen thousand subscribers as an apology. Sales are through the roof, systems are functional, and Dad can go eat a pile of monkey dung." That little condition for getting Mom's engagement ring didn't work. I bested Dad.

She gives me a half-pleased, half-sick look. "Can we talk about something other than poop?"

I squeeze her hand and laugh.

As the limo stops in from of the sleek silver and glass building, she smiles.

"The MOMA! I've never been." Her smile dazzles me as we enter the Museum of Modern Art.

"I know." We get out and enter like everyone else, though I have a membership card. When your family donates the equivalent of the GDP of a small island nation to the arts, you get free admission and ten percent off the gift shop like everyone else.

We walk in, bookshelves and brochure racks everywhere, and I take Shannon past all of it, to the right, pressing the button for the fifth floor on the elevator panel.

"What are you doing?" she asks, puzzled yet intrigued. Her earnest brown eyes search mine, and she squeezes my hand. Mom's ring rests in my front pocket now, no longer needing to be hidden. Shannon knows I want to make this right, to propose and ask her to marry me, but she doesn't quite know the particulars.

But you can be damn sure there won't be tiramisu within a hundred feet of us.

Years have passed since I've been here, but the route is ingrained, an invisible hand guiding me.

"Wait! Dec, I want to look at—" Shannon objects as we fly by other paintings.

"We will. Trust me," I say back, squeezing her hand.

"Is this some special speed tour? Like speed dating, but for the MOMA? Ten seconds per painting?" she jokes.

We turn a corner and then there we are.

The Van Gogh gallery.

I stop so fast that Shannon bumps into me from behind, her body soft and yielding. I've become a brick wall, shrouded by a supernatural sensation, an eerie feeling that is a combination of deja vu, grief, and pure joy. My muscles pulse and my heart begins to beat so fast it feels like my chest shudders. I'm numb and on fire, cold and tense. At ease and alive.

I can feel her here. My mother. Her ring is in my pocket and her soul is smiling on us.

Maybe Shannon will get a chance to meet her after all.

"Honey, what's wrong?" Shannon asks, turning me toward her, hands on my cheeks. All I can do is blink. Senses on fire, ears perked for sound, it's as if I can hear her if I just focus enough. Feel her. Call her.

My eyes catch on the painting that is my destination and I take one step toward it, then two, holding Shannon's hand and bringing her there. My hand crushes hers but she doesn't flinch, her purposeful strides matching mine. She does not question me now. She only follows.

And there it is.

We stop, captivated, Shannon's eyes on the painting.

But mine are on her.

And there, in front of tourists wearing earbuds to listen to guided tours in their native language, amidst parents with toddlers in backpacks and elderly people in wheelchairs, in the swirling pleasure of humanity in every shade, every voice, every belief, I drop down to one knee, Mom's ring already in my palm before I look up at Shannon's beautiful face, and I say her name.

"Shannon."

A hush fills the already-quiet gallery.

"I came here as a boy on the edge of manhood with my mother. We stood in front of this very painting, and she told me that one day I would find my morning star. The yin to my yang. The love of my life."

She pulls her fingers to her mouth, covering her lips, and tears fill her eyes, a shaky smile making her ethereal.

"You are the star that lights up my darkest nights. You are the sun that I revolve around. We met in a men's room—"

The hush becomes a series of troubled murmurs in the background, and Shannon laughs, then sniffs.

"—and you nearly broke my penis on our first date—"

The crowd around us gets bigger. Shannon's openly laughing now.

"And I wouldn't have it any other way. My life before I met you was neat and orderly. I had all the control. All the power. My world made sense and if it didn't, I *made* it make sense. What I didn't have was any of the love, Shannon." My voice catches, wobbling as I say her name. "You brought back love."

"Oh, Declan," she says, bending down, eyes filled with tears, searching my face.

I'm determined to do this just right, and swallow, hard.

"You brought the love that I needed, even when I had no idea I was living with a hollow hole where my heart should be. That I've been living half alive without you and thinking I was complete."

I hold up the ring.

"You have the other half of my heart, my love. And I think I have yours. Will you marry me, Shannon, so we can be whole, together?"

The crowd gasps, collectively holding their breath. I'm right there with them.

And then:

"Oh, yes, oh *yes yes yes*," she whispers as I slide the ring on her left ring finger.

It fits perfectly.

I stand and we kiss on the shining floor of the gallery on that fifth floor at the MOMA, a security guard clearing his throat, the crowd around us applauding and calling out congratulations.

I can't hear any of them, though, over the sound of our hearts beating in sync.

* * *

We take our time. Shannon's fingers move slowly over the buttons of my shirt, soundlessly opening me to her touch. Moonlight bounces off the diamond resting in its platinum setting, her left hand weighed down by the newness of the ring. The thin band of metal is cold against my bare chest, the sensation making me sigh as her palm slides under my shirt, following the planes of my body.

Another button, another breath, another look. She kisses me on the breastbone, then over my heart, my own hands gentle at her waist, my body primed to make love yet held in check.

We have all night.

We have all our lives.

"Thank you," she murmurs against the soft skin of my neck, just under my ear.

"For what?"

"For loving me."

My breath catches. "I never had a choice."

In the open room we're two bodies, two hearts pumping blood, four lungs exchanging air, four eyes and hands taking in the terrain of each other's body. Her lips on my neck are the sweetest movement, my hands finding her hot skin and sliding up the rolling hills of her breasts, the supple silk of her nipples as they tighten like sculpting desire with my own hands.

The suite I booked is all clean lines and dark wood, dim lights and wide windows, thirty-nine floors above the city and the bed is as big as a small field. We undress each other, the clothes pooling at our feet with whispers and the hushed sound of gravity at work. Soon we're nude, bare before each other in all our glory, and her eyes captivate me.

Slow blues music plays in the background as I pull her into my arms, thighs embedded between hers, the curvature of her spine against my forearms like it was hand-carved to fit my grasp. Her lips and tongue meet mine with abandon, love so different now, forged in commitment and declaration, in promises and—soon—vows.

I *asked*. She said *yes*.

Now we show each other how true it all is.

My wanting has a new tone, a different tenor, changed irreparably by my proposal, her acceptance, our joining. At home, wanting Shannon took on a crude sort of steamy demand, like a second set of veins and arteries in me, a pulse that could only be tamed by sex.

What I feel now is so wholly changed that I cannot call it the same. This is sultry. Mature. Ripe and lush, a give and take that is less about quenching a need and more about tending a flame. She dances in my arms, a slow, languid journey we've only just begun.

"I love you," she whispers against my mouth.

"I know."

We recline on the bed, hands slow in their ministrations, achingly aware of everything. So many times I've made love with Shannon and never noticed the arch of her thigh, this small mole on her hip, the way she bites her lip when I kiss here *there*.

How could I have missed so much that has been right in front of me all this time?

"We're really doing this."

She doesn't mean making love. "We are, Mrs. McCormick." My own words make me shiver. She joins me.

Her hand spreads against my navel, fingers hooking one by one against my skin. "I like the sound of that."

I slide one hand to a place where her pleasure often starts. She grinds against me and makes a thick sound from her throat.

"And I like the sound of *that*," I say as I dip *down, down, down* to a place where I won't hear more than the coursing of blood through her body, twinned with mine in rhythm.

The only place in the world I want to be.

Minutes later she pulls me up, sweat lingering between her breasts, begging to be licked away. Her mouth is fast on mine, urgent and pleading. Her thighs part and a steady hand takes me home.

The second I'm in her she opens her eyes, staring up with a depth that makes me see other dimensions.

Layers of love. The faces of children we have not dreamed of yet.

And the unfolding of the rest of my life.

We make love with our bodies, striving to match with flesh what we see in each other's souls.

We fail.

Guess we'll just have to try again.

And again and again and again.

For the next sixty or so years.

'Til death do us part.

CHAPTER EIGHTEEN

The Momzilla...

Someone's using a mirror to reflect the sun on my face, like I'm an ant under a magnifying glass. The pinpoint of heat on my cheekbone is maddening. I crack one eye open and shut it, fast, before I'm blinded.

Not a magnifying glass.

That's Shannon's diamond.

It's morning in NYC, the muted sounds of traffic outside below us a backdrop for the day after the best day of my life. Shannon's next to me, warm and soft, brown hair a tousled mess and stretched across my chest like tentacles claiming me.

Her mouth is open in a half smile, as if she's dreaming happy thoughts, and in repose she is ethereal. Otherworldly. Soft and vulnerable.

And she's *mine*.

I'm hers right back, too. We're each other's love, and in a year and a half or so, we'll make it official. The wedding, the license, the piece of paper that deems us legally husband and wife isn't that important. It's a symbol.

We're already joined.

We've been joined since the day I found her with her hand in that damn toilet.

Love at first flush.

She moves, rolling over and rubbing her eyes, a shaft of strong sunlight shining in her face. Unlike me, she doesn't get a tiny tan from it reflecting off a prism. Her face moves toward me, arms wrapping around my neck, ring hand sinking into my hair and cupping the back of my head as we give each other a morning kiss that makes me seek out her warmth.

The kiss breaks and she whispers:

"We have to tell my parents. Your dad, too."

I groan, the feeling a rebel cry from my fellow men throughout the ages, stretching back to the dawn of time, to cavemen past with mothers-in-law who drove them nuts, too. I'll bet all those cave drawings aren't of wooly mammoths being stabbed with spears. If you look close enough, they're mothers-in-law.

"I thought waiting for the ring to, uh, come out was the worst part of all this, but Marie? Planning our wedding? You're killing me."

"Just get us into Farmington Country Club and she'll be happy." She waves the ring around in the sunlight, a tiny white spot jiggling on the ceiling and walls like a very expensive laser pointer. If Chuckles were here he'd be a furry ping-pong ball, trying to catch it.

"Your mother will need her own reality television show. Momzilla. She'll make Bridezillas cringe in fear."

Shannon laughs. I don't think she realizes how serious I am. "It'll be fine," Shannon insists, cuddling up against me, her creamy thigh nudging up along mine, knee headed toward my hipbone. That lush warmth drives all thoughts of Marie away and makes me think maybe this wedding won't be so bad after all.

Shannon's phone buzzes again. She sighs, and the thigh disappears as she gets up. While I like the warm skin on mine and miss it, the view of her ass is spectacular. A guy could get used to seeing that every day for the rest of his life.

My throat closes.

I will get to see that ass every day. For the rest of my life.

How did I get so lucky?

"It's Mom," Shannon says, reading her phone. "She wants to know if we can get a cake topper with a woman's hand in a toilet and a guy in a suit giving her the thumb's up."

I groan again.

Millions of men through time and space groan with me. I'll need their support.

"And Agnes wants an invitation, too."

This is going to be a long process.

Shannon says something into the phone and I hear Marie's scream of joy. The two speak in fast-forward breakneck speed, until Shannon calls out,

"Honey? What do you look like in a kilt?"

I have no idea, but I have a sinking feeling I'm about to find out. At my own wedding.

A single kiss on Shannon's shoulder makes her giggle. As I cup her breast with one wanting hand, she stifles a moan. Marie's voice chatters on, dominated mostly by three words: Farmington, helicopter and kilt.

I don't want to know.

Peeling Shannon off the phone turns out to be easier than expected when she tells Marie to call Farmington and book it.

Click.

"I need coffee," Shannon declares, looking around the room. She pads off to the bathroom. I walk over to the balcony and look out over Central Park. The view is spectacular.

I look at Shannon.

Even better.

My own phone buzzes suddenly.

"You need to answer that."

"No, I don't."

Shannon pokes her head out from the bathroom. "Yes, you do. It could be your dad."

"Why would my dad call me? He has nineteen-year-old assistants to do that, and they just call Grace, who calls me."

"It could be Grace, then." I crawl back into bed, determined to ignore my phone.

"Hey! There's no coffee in this hotel room!" Shannon shouts from across the room. "What kind of fancy hotel doesn't have a coffeemaker in it?"

They assume you'll order room service, but instead of explaining, I seize my chance because I'm a guy, and that's what we do.

"You'll just have to help me wake up the same way you did back home that one morning," I say, holding the sheet up so she can crawl under.

"What about me?"

"I'm happy to wake you up that way, too."

She laughs, a throaty sound that makes me tent the sheets. "*That* makes me sleepy, Dec. Caffeine is what I need."

"I promise that my wake-up method will not put you to sleep." I leer at her. "If not that, how about a nice bath in the tub? I'll soap you up. You're a dirty girl."

BZZZZ.

She reaches for my phone and tosses it at me. It's Grace. I answer.

"I'm just going to take off my makeup," Shannon says from the bathroom doorway.

"Don't take too long!" I call back. "I can't wait to soap you up." I wave her off and turn my attention to the phone.

"Hi Grace."

"Declan, I'm sorry to bother you, but Shannon's mother is on the phone requesting that we reserve the corporate helicopter, a jet, and a yacht for an unspecified date in 2016. Does Anterdec even have a yacht? And what does she mean when she says she needs fifty bagpipe players and a dozen kilt tuxedoes made from McCormick tartan as well?"

And Shannon wonders why I have Resting Asshole Face.

Epilogue (sort of)

Shannon

"I'm just going to take off my make-up," I shout out to the main room as I slip into the bathroom. Behind me is a jacuzzi bathtub bigger than the neighborhood pool I swam in as a kid. Geez—this place can have a tub like that but can't bother with a basic Keurig machine in the room?

Barbarians.

"Don't take too long!" Declan calls back. "I can't wait to soap you up." He's just proposed (heh—I love that word) a long, hot soak in the tub and I suspect Declan has plans to make a certain part of his anatomy a loofah for a certain part of mine.

My reflection smiles back at me, cheeks pink and eyes as glowing as polished amber. Mrs. Declan McCormick. Shannon Jacoby McCormick.

Declan's wife.

I grab the bottle of eye make-up remover and smear some on a tissue, working the mascara off. It's that new kind, where you use three different gels and one tube of loose fibers that look like ground up cockroach legs and then some pixie dust made from an eleventh century druid's secret alchemist's box.

But I end up with eyelashes that make me look like a character in a Hayao Miyazaki movie, so it's worth it.

One eye done, I move on to the other eye and really goop on the eye makeup remover. My ring glitters in the light and I can't stop smiling. I just can't. The ring is perfect, no matter where it's been.

And this ring has *been* places...

As I finish my second eye, a chunk of mascara is stubborn. More eye makeup remover and a lot of rubbing and it's free. Whew. I reach for more tissues, wipe my eyes, and then wipe the extra off my hands.

The ring slips off as I'm cleaning my palm, flying high in an eerily familiar arc as I scream "Noooooooooooooooooooo" like I'm in slow motion, the platinum circle plunking into the toilet and rotating, diamond down, weighted by three carats of *holy shit*.

"Shannon? You okay?" Declan calls out. I ignore him.

The toilet has automatic flush. If I don't get there in time—

My hand goes straight in the water and my fingers are slippery with that waterproof eye makeup remover petroleum product crap that I curse a thousand times as I try to get the ring. I feel like the Gollum. My precious.

My precious......

I did not endure #Poopwatch for three days, defile a French fry tray, and endure countless poop jokes from every man I know between the ages of six and fifty-three (which is *every* man I know) to have the ring going down the sewer pipes and into the Hudson River because I was removing *makeup*.

The irony of that is not lost on me.

The door bursts open and Declan is standing there, completely naked, a fine and glorious specimen of a man. He crosses his arms over his chest and leans against the doorway, hot, sculpted ass propping him.

"You lied," is all he says as my fingers work to find the ring.

"Huh?" My brain halts but those fingers are determined.

"You said you didn't have a hand-in-the-toilet fetish. Is this a joke?" he says, laughing. "Playing a little prank? Reliving how we met?"

When he laughs, things...bounce. It's distracting. It's incredibly droolworthy, too. The ring I'm scrambling to grab is a symbol of his commitment to let me touch the bouncy stuff whenever I want.

C'mon ring. Don't fail me now.

His face changes when I don't answer and he stands up, walking to the toilet, staring down. "No phone?"

I shake my head.

"No vibrator?"

I shake my head.

"No fetal pink pig?"

I shake my head.

"Then what's so important that you would—*oh, don't you dare tell me you dropped the Goddamn ring in there!*" Declan bellows.

He really does know me a little too well.

And just then, the toilet flushes automatically.

He takes one more step and he's looking down at my arm directly, fist in the bottom of the bowl as the water gurgles and swirls around me. The water sprays up and a thin mist of—yes—toilet water covers my makeupless face.

He mutters something under his breath in Russian, some kind of curse words. It turns me on. I *really* don't want to be turned on while I have my hand in a toilet. The brain makes strange associations and I'd rather not have my erotic dreams for the next few months involve this scenario.

Again.

The flush fades and we're left in silence, me with a disgusting, germy face and my arm still so deep in the toilet I might as well be helping a cow give birth.

"You *do* have the ring," he says slowly, eyes narrowing as he crouches next to me. The light layer of dark hair all over his muscled thighs makes me want to be naked and dirty with him. I can't help myself.

A different kind of dirty...

I slowly pull my hand out of the toilet, fist tight, and reach out within inches of his face. Unfurling my fingers one by one, his creased brow relaxes.

The light bounces off the three-carat diamond.

And the, uh, droplets of germ-filled water.

His nostrils twitch and one side of his mouth twists up in a smile as he says, "Toilet Girl."

"Hot Guy," I say back, eyes racing over him as he laughs. Oh, please, keep laughing. I love the view.

"You are crazy, Shannon."

"That's why you love me," I say as I stand and wash my hands.

248

"I love you because you stick your hand down toilet bowls?"

"No, you love me because I'm *willing* to stick my hand down toilet bowls."

He's looking at me with the same expression he reserves for my mother. "Parse that one out. Does not compute."

"Why do you love me?" I ask, throwing the question back at him.

"Why do I breathe?"

Oh, this man.

He bends over and turns on the water for the bathtub, the pounding sound filling the tiny room. The faucet is as strong as a firehose. The rich really do live different lives. They even have different plumbing.

I slide the ring back on my finger and breathe a sigh of relief.

His arms envelop me and our nude skin touches everywhere it can.

"I'm covered in toilet water," I protest as he comes in for a kiss.

"Not the first time." He kisses me even as I cringe. It's not a very good kiss.

"Dec—who was that on the phone?"

"Grace."

"Everything okay?"

"It was about your mom."

I sigh. "What's she done now?"

"She wants Grace to start ordering McCormick tartan plaid for the dozen kilt tuxedoes. And she'd like to commandeer Air Force One."

I close my eyes and bite my lip, the rush of the inevitable filling my cotton-headed brain. "This is how she's starting?" I ask in disbelief. "Ten minutes after I call her?"

"You expected less? She'll ask Robert Kraft for Gillette Stadium for the rehearsal party next." He bends slightly, hand in the water. His arm hooks behind my knees and I'm in his arms, then unceremoniously tossed into the half-full tub like it's Spring Break and we're poolside in Cancun.

I scream with laughter and shock as the water assaults me. Declan follows it, hungry hands and mouth everywhere.

Bzzzz.

"Don't answer that!" we shout in unison.

And we don't.

Hours later, Declan orders room service and I finally get my coffee. Caffeine deprivation leaves me wondering which is worse: the pounding in my head or the pounding in my—

On the tray there is a pot of coffee and a dozen chocolate covered strawberries, half milk chocolate, half dark.

And, oddly enough, a bowl of chocolate-covered pretzels mixed with cheese curls.

Declan walks into the bathroom with the room service cart as I survey it and give him a questioning look. He drops the robe he threw on hastily and stands there, offering me a cup of coffee while my pruney toes turn the hot water back on.

Look at him.

Really look at him.

Is this bathroom aesthetically pleasing?

Oh, yeah.

THE END

* * *

If you haven't read Declan and Shannon's story in the *Shopping for a Billionaire Boxed Set*, go read it right now! This series began in May 2014 as a serial, and the boxed set has 670+ pages of their hilarious, hot, and crazy story.

Read more now!

Shopping for a Billionaire Boxed Set

* * *

Wondering if Amanda and Andrew have something going on?
Oh, yeah....

Here's a sneak peak of *Shopping for a CEO*, which starts with a Prologue that takes place at the same time Declan broke up with Shannon in the *Shopping for a Billionaire Boxed Set*.
Shannon's best friend Amanda takes on Andrew McCormick when she crashes his office and demands his help in bringing Shannon and Declan together.
What she doesn't count on is finding her hot anger morphing into a hot attraction...

"What the hell is wrong with your stupid brother?" I shout as I barge into Andrew McCormick's office. For the past few years I've worked with Anterdec in some capacity, but I've never been in here before. The office is huge. The windows are so broad and the view of the ocean so good that if you hold a folder up just below your eyes to block out the tops of the buildings you can think you're at sea.

I hold back from doing that because I don't want to look like a freak. My mother's constant mantra fills my mind: *Don't draw attention to yourself, Amanda.*

Kind of hard to avoid doing that when you barge unannounced into a CEO's office, but I don't need to make it worse.

"Well, hello there, Amanda," he says with a weird, surprised smile. "What's Terry done now?" he adds with a sigh. "I told him he couldn't legally marry two women at once, even in Vegas -- "

"Not *that* brother! Declan!" Though suddenly I find myself very intrigued by this little factoid about Terrance McCormick.

"Nothing's wrong with Declan." Could Andrew be any more smug? There's such a look of boredom, like I'm a pest, and it's the eyebrow lift that challenges me. The crossed arms over pecs that swell evenly, up and down, like a metronome in half time. The sinewy tendons in those arms, covered with a smattering of golden hair. Smug. Right.

Why am I here again? It's not just to wipe away drool.

Oh, yeah. Shannon. Shannon and her douchebag ex...not-ex...whatever you call Declan. Steve holds the official title of Shannon's Douchebag Ex, so I have to think of something new for Declan. Billionaire Douchebag Ex has a nice ring to it.

Billionaire Asshat Douchebag is even better.

"Your brother is being a complete asshole to Shannon and breaking her heart," I snap. Andrew needs to be outraged. He needs to react. He needs to understand the gravity of the situation.

But no.

"Maybe she should have thought about that when she pretended to be your wife and lied to Declan," he says flatly, staring hard at my breasts, and not my eyes. What is it with this guy? My bosom betrays me, confusing my anger for arousal, and suddenly a red creeping flush covers the top of my chest. I look like a blushing porn actress.

Let me explain the "your wife" comment. I'm not gay. My best friend Shannon is not gay. We're mystery shoppers, which, if you're a fellow mystery shopper, explains *everything*.

You're not? Oh.

"Lied?" I seize on the one word that pierces the sudden forcefield that surrounds us, making it impossible to focus on anything other than his thick, wavy hair, glittering blue eyes that alternate between cold and hot....

"She lied to him," he says in a neutral tone, blasé and casual, like he's all *Whatev* and I'm all *ERMIGERD!*

"My best friend did not lie!"

"You breast friend...I mean *best* friend, most certainly did." His mouth is set firmly, but those eyes are dancing.

I snort. He's looking at my rack like he's on the sinking Titanic and these are the floatation devices.

I look at him -- *really* look at him -- for the first time, and gasp.

"Why are you wearing bicycle shorts?" I hiss. They're so form fitting I can tell not only that he's circumcised, but given enough time I could probably research which OB did it based on technique.

His hair is slightly damp as he runs a calm hand through it and flashes me a lopsided grin. "You caught me after my spin class." The way a stray wave rests against his strong brow, how those eyes shine out from under thick eyebrows and glimmer with mirth.

And a little smoke and heat. It's as if...

"You didn't shower in the gym?" I choke out, realizing *he's* watching *me* stare at *him*. And he doesn't have a rack to ogle.

He points to a stationary bike in the corner. "No gym. The trainer comes here." He points to a door. "The shower is in there." There's that lopsided smile again, and his eyes go to...

Yep.

"You know my eyes are up here," I say pointedly.

He looks at them. "They're very pretty."

"Thank you." Wait. I cannot be distracted by a sweaty, musky, hot man who is staring at my rack.

Okay, I can be. In fact, if I weren't distracted by that, I'd be made of stone.

* * *

Shopping for a CEO is coming in 2015. Join my newsletter mailing list or Facebook page to stay tuned for release dates.

OTHER BOOKS BY JULIA KENT

Suggested Reading Order

Shopping for a Billionaire: The Collection (Parts 1-5 in one bundle, 670 pages!)
- Shopping for a Billionaire 1
- Shopping for a Billionaire 2
- Shopping for a Billionaire 3
- Shopping for a Billionaire 4
- Christmas Shopping for a Billionaire

Shopping for a Billionaire's Fiancée

Before Her Billionaires
Her Billionaires: Boxed Set (Parts 1-4 in one bundle, 458 pages!)
- Her First Billionaire—FREE
- Her Second Billionaire
- Her Two Billionaires
- Her Two Billionaires and a Baby

It's Complicated
Complete Abandon (A Her Billionaires novella)
Complete Harmony (A Her Billionaires novella #2)
Complete Bliss (A Her Billionaires novella #3)
Complete We (A Her Billionaires novella #4)

SHOPPING FOR A BILLIONAIRE'S FIANCÉE

ABOUT THE AUTHOR

Text JKentBooks to 77948 and get a text message on release dates!

New York Times and *USA Today* bestselling author Julia Kent turned to writing contemporary romance after deciding that life is too short not to have fun. She writes romantic comedy with an edge, and new adult books that push contemporary boundaries. From billionaires to BBWs to rock stars, Julia finds a sensual, goofy joy in every book she writes, but unlike Trevor from *Random Acts of Crazy*, she has never kissed a chicken.

She loves to hear from her readers by email at jkentauthor@gmail.com, on Twitter @jkentauthor, and on Facebook at facebook.com/jkentauthor
Visit her website at http://jkentauthor.com

18152356R00161

Made in the USA
Middletown, DE
24 February 2015